A TREASURY OF
FUNNY
STORIES

KINGFISHER
Larousse Kingfisher Chambers Inc.
95 Madison Avenue
New York, New York 10016

First American edition 1995
2 4 6 8 10 9 7 5 3 1

Library of Congress Cataloging-in-Publication Data
A Treasury of Funny stories/compiled by Andrew Matthews
illustrated by Frank James.
—1st American ed.
p. cm.
1. Children's stories, American. 2. Children's stories, English
3. Humorous stories, American. 4. Humorous stories, English.
[1. Short stories. 2. Humorous stories.]
I. Matthews, Andrew, - II. James, Frank, - ill.
PZ5. T752 1995 94-30242
813'.01089282—dc20 CIP AC

ISBN 1-85697-544-4
Printed in Portugal

A TREASURY OF
FUNNY
STORIES

Chosen by
ANDREW MATTHEWS

Illustrated by
FRANK JAMES

Kingfisher
NEW YORK

CONTENTS

DOCTOR BOOX AND THE SORE GIRAFFE

Andrew Davies

My friend Doctor Boox, the animal doctor, lives in a big house with rather a lot of animals: dogs, cats, lizards, goats, and so on. Doctor Boox is not the cleverest man in the world, but he does his best. Well: this is the story about Boox and the sore giraffe.

One morning, rather late, Doctor Boox was lying in bed with a few dogs and hamsters, when the telephone rang.

"Boox here," said Boox. "What do you want?"

"Schmitt itty Shoo Shah," said the telephone.

"Can't hear a word you're saying," said Boox. This was because he had his stethoscope stuck in his ears. He always kept it there to be on the safe side. He took it off and gave it to a dog to hold.

7

"This is the Zoo," said the telephone. "We've got a sore giraffe here."

"Where is it sore?" said Boox.

"In the neck," said the man on the telephone.

"Oh dear," said Boox. "I was afraid of that."

"Well, can you help?"

"Oh, I'll have a go," said Boox. He put the phone down.

"Right lads," said Boox to the dogs. "We're off to the Zoo."

"Row! Row! Row!" shouted the dogs.

They went downstairs to Doctor Boox's red

sports car and they all got in. Three of the dogs sat on Boox's knee. "Move over lads," said Boox. "Let the dog see the rabbit." And then they were off. Boox drove very fast because it was an emergency.

On the way, he had an idea. He was no fool, and as he had not had dealings with any giraffes before, he thought he would practice on a lamppost. So he parked his car by one of the biggest lamp-posts in town.

"Let's see," said Boox. And he took a quick run at the lamppost and went up it in three jumps and a scramble.

"Easy!" said Boox. "Pretty good, eh lads?" But when he looked down at the dogs in the car they seemed a long way down and Doctor Boox began to get frightened. He clung very tight to the lamppost.

"Row! Row! Row!" shouted the dogs. They wanted him to get down, but Boox didn't know how to get down.

Just then, a policeman came along. "What are you doing up there?" he said.

"Training," said Boox. "I've got to get up a giraffe this morning."

"A likely tale," said the police-man. "Get down at once!"

"I can't," said Boox. "I'm frightened." So the policeman went away and got the fire brigade.

Soon the red fire engine came along. "I thought you were never coming," said Boox.

The firemen hoisted the big ladder, and Boox stepped very carefully onto it. "Thanks very much," he said. Then he had another idea.

"I'll tell you what," he said. "What about taking me to the Zoo?"

"All right," said the fireman, who had nothing better to do that morning.

So all the dogs got in the fire engine, and the firemen drove to the Zoo, with Boox still on the ladder.

"This is the life," said Boox to himself, as they whizzed through the town with the bells ringing.

When they got to the Zoo they drove straight up to the giraffe, who was very sore indeed now, and rather cross. But Boox got out his bottle of liniment (on the label it said:

DOCTOR BOOX'S
DOUBLE STRENGTH
NECK RUB)

and rubbed the giraffe's neck with it. After a bit the giraffe said:

"Ahhhhh."

"He's better now," said Boox.

"Thank you very much," said the Zoo man.

"Good old Boox," said the firemen.

"Row! Row! Row!" said the dogs.

"Don't mention it," said Boox. "Anybody like to come back to my house for a snack?"

They all got into the fire engine and went back to Doctor Boox's house where they all had lemonade and three cookies each out of Doctor Boox's big cookie jar.

Except Boox.

Boox had five cookies because he thought he owed it to himself after his busy morning.

CRUMMY MUMMY

Anne Fine

I don't think my mum's fit to be a parent, really I don't. Every morning it's the same, every single morning. I'm standing by the front door with my coat on, ready to go. School starts at nine and it's already eight-forty or even later, and she's not ready. She's not even nearly ready. Sometimes she isn't even dressed.

"Come *on*," I shout up the stairs. "We have to leave now."

"Hang on a minute!"

"What are you *doing* up there?"

Her voice comes, all muffled, through the bedroom door:

"Nothing."

"You *must* be doing something," I yell.

"I'm *not*."

12

"Come down, then. We're *waiting*."

"Can't find my shoes."

I lean against the front door, sighing. With as much patience as I can muster, I call upstairs:

"Where did you take them off?"

"I *thought* I took them off in the bathroom . . ."

"Look there, then."

"I *have*."

"If you would only put your shoes away neatly at night, we wouldn't have to go through this every single morning!"

By now, of course, my baby sister's fretting. She's strapped inside her push-chair and since I put her coat and bonnet on at least ten minutes ago, and she's still indoors, her head and ears are getting hot and scratchy. She's boiling up into one of her little rages. Already she's trying to tug her bonnet off.

"Will you come *on*?" I shout upstairs. (I'm really getting mad now.)

"I'm coming. I'm coming!"

"Well, hurry *up*!"

At last, she comes downstairs. And even then

she's never dressed right. You'd think, honestly you would, that we didn't have any windows upstairs, the way she chooses what to wear. She certainly can't bother to look through them at the weather. She'll sail down in midwinter, when it's snowing, in a thin cotton frock with short puffy sleeves, and no woolly.

I have to be firm.

"You can't come out like that."

"Why not?"

"You just can't," I tell her. "You'll catch your death. It's snowing out there. It's *far* too cold for bare arms. You'll freeze."

"I'll put a coat on."

But I just stare at her until she goes back upstairs for a sweater. And even then she'll choose something quite unsuitable. She never dresses in the right sort of thing. She'd wear her glittery leg warmers to a funeral if I let her (or if we ever went to funerals). She'd sit on a beach in her thick purple pon-cho. If she were called in to see the headmaster, she'd rather wear those baggy flowery shorts she found abandoned on a park bench last Easter than anything sensible. She'd look fantastic—she always does—but not at all like a mother. You have to watch her. You can't let up.

At least she admits it.

"I'm a terrible embarrassment to you, Minna," she confesses, buckling on two of her best studded belts. "I'm a Crummy Mummy."

Then I feel mean for being so stern.

"You're not a Crummy Mummy," I tell her. "You do your best. And I suppose it doesn't *really* matter what you look like . . ."

"You're right," she says, cheering up at once. And then, if you let her, she'd get worse. At least, that's what my gran says, and she should know because she's her mother.

I like my gran. She lives right on the other side of the estate, but she comes over almost every teatime. She picks Miranda out of the cot, and coos to her, and then she sits with Miranda on her knee on the only bit of the sofa that isn't leaking stuffing. Mostly, she tells Mum off. She says now Mum's a mother of two, it's time she grew up and pulled herself together. She tells Mum she should throw all her safety-pin earrings and lavender fishnet tights into the dustbin, and go out and buy herself a nice, decent frock from Marks and Spencers. She says Mum ought to take those horrible Punk Skunks records off the stereo before they ruin Miranda, and put something nice and easy to listen to, like Perry Como's Christmas Selection.

And then, if Mum hasn't already flounced off in a huff, Gran purses her lips together as if she's been sucking lemons and, clutching Miranda so tightly her dummy pops out of her mouth and her face goes purple, she whispers to Mum that she's clearly still very much under the influence of that dreadful, *dreadful*—

Here, she looks around shiftily, and drops her voice even lower:

"I don't even want to say his *name* in front of innocent children, but you know exactly who I mean."

I know exactly who she means, too. She means Crusher Maggot, that's who she means.

Crusher Maggot is Mum's boyfriend. It was me who first called him Crusher Maggot because that's what he looks like, and when he first started coming round here I didn't like him. Now I like him a lot, but it's too late. The nickname's stuck. He doesn't mind, though. And now even Mum calls him Crusher Maggot.

Gran disapproves of Crusher. She thinks he's

a very bad influence on Mum. She blames him for giving Miranda her nickname—Crummy Dummy—and she particularly hates his hair. She says it's a hideous embarrassment.

Crusher's hair is fantastic. He even won a punk hair competition with it once, and his photo ended up on one of those London postcards that tourists send home to their friends for a laugh. The postcard was called *London's Burning*. And there's our Crusher, teeth bared, eyes staring, his hair in flaming red and orange spikes, scowling horribly at the photographer. We've got it propped up on the mantelpiece. Gran hates the sight of it.

But, then again, when Crusher goes to all the trouble of shaving his head, Gran doesn't like that any better. She doesn't like his tattoo. I've even heard her telling our next-door neighbors how common she thinks it is. And they agreed. (They're not keen on Crusher, either. They don't like the noise his car makes when it starts—*if* it starts. They say it wakes their children.)

Personally, I rather like Crusher's tattoo. It only shows up when his head is freshly shaved. It says MADE IN BIRMINGHAM, and

17

Crusher claims he was—well, on the outskirts. And we don't see it all that often anyway, because whenever he's gone to the trouble of dyeing his hair a different color, he lets the spikes grow out all over.

Crusher dyes his hair pretty often, considering. Since the postcard, he's been green and pink, yellow and purple. Right now, he's blue. Gran and he had a row about it only last week. Crusher just happened to stroll into the kitchen while Gran was tipping breakfast plates into the sink and washing them, so we could start on tea. Mum was upstairs, doing something in the bathroom, no one knew what, but it was using up all the hot water, Gran said. And I was giving Crummy Dummy her bottle.

"Wotcha, Granny," Crusher greeted her cheerily. "I hope one of those plates you're rinsing is for me."

He's ever so friendly, is Crusher Maggot. I can't think why Gran just can't get used to him, like I did. But she can't. She spun round at the draining board and glowered at him before saying tartly:

"You've got your feet well and truly under the table, haven't you, young Maggot?"

Baffled, Crusher looked down at his Doc Martins. But Gran kept on at him. She's good at nagging, Gran is. (Mum says that I take after her.)

18

"Look at your hair!" Gran snorted. "It's sky blue! It's dreadful the way you amble around this estate looking like something that fell off the wall at a modern art gallery. I'm horrified that a daughter of mine is prepared even to be seen walking along the street beside someone with hair that shocking color!"

"Your hair is blue, too," argued Crusher. He was hurt. "You had that perm and rinse and set only last week. Your hair is definitely blue."

"A faint bluish tinge, maybe," Gran said, blushing hotly. "Not sky blue!"

"Not royal blue, either!" I cried. For Mum had just sailed into the kitchen. And her hair was royal blue! It was the brightest, deepest, richest blue I ever saw. It was bluer than winter afternoons, bluer than the leggings Gran knitted for Crummy Dummy, bluer even than Sophie Howard's gown when she played the Virgin Mary in our Nativity play last year.

Gran stared. I stared. Crusher stared. Even Crummy Dummy stared. Then Gran and

Crummy Dummy both burst into tears.

"Waaaah!" screamed Crummy Dummy, and she stretched out her arms desperately to me, hoping I would protect her from this blue-topped stranger.

"Aaaaagh!" shrieked poor Gran, holding her hand over her heart. Gingerly, she stuck out a finger and prodded one of Mum's spikes.

"How can you do this to your old mother?" she wailed. "A girl's hair is supposed to be her crowning glory! Royal blue hair! *Royal blue hair!* What will the neighbors think? Answer me that!"

"They'll think she looks fair smashing," said Crusher. "And that she matches the paintwork on my car."

You could tell Gran was shocked. She went pale as a grub.

"I'm warning you two," she said in her dangerous voice. "You're going too far. A mother can only stand *so much*."

(This interested me. A lot. For I suspect my mum can stand almost any amount. It's me who cracks. That's why I have a lot of natural sympathy for my gran.)

Gran shook her finger at Mum so hard that her new perm and set wobbled on her head like a pale blue jelly.

"If you stay royal blue, I shall disown you.

Yes, I shall. I won't come round here anymore. I won't babysit for you when you go down to the disco with this—this *barbarian* here" (pointing at Crusher, who looked hurt again). "I won't talk to you. I'll even cut you dead in the street. You have to choose. Royal blue hair, or your own mother!"

There was a horrible silence. Nobody moved. Nobody spoke. Mum just looked sulky.

Gran turned to me. Prising Crummy Dummy out of my arms, she placed a kiss upon her forehead.

"Farewell, sweet babe," she said. "I hope for your sake that your mother sees sense, and we are not parted for too long."

I got a kiss and a speech too.

"Goodbye, Minna dear," she said "I know it can be hard when a mother puts maggots before the family."

I had some sympathy with that, as well. I've thought it often enough myself, when Mum and Crusher are too wrapped up in giggling together about something silly to pay any attention to me.

"'Bye, Gran," I said. "I, too, hope our parting won't last for long."

It did, though. It lasted for days. Gran never visited once. I was pretty upset, I can tell you. I missed her coming over every afternoon and asking me about what happened at school, and helping me with my spelling homework. And Crummy Dummy missed her too, you could tell. She took to sitting forlornly with her dummy in her mouth, looking all miserable and deprived.

On Wednesday, we caught sight of Gran for the first time since the quarrel. She was stepping out of Mr. Hamid's shop carrying a bagful of vegetables just as we came over the pedestrian walkway to the shopping center. I waved and shouted at her through the railings; but since I was with Mum, Gran ignored me and swept off under the concrete arches extremely grandly, like the Queen Mother, pretending she hadn't heard me call.

"See where your stubbornness has led us?" I scolded Mum, as Gran disappeared between Vikki's Video Palace and the boarded-up wool shop.

Mum said something rude. I shan't repeat it. But I persisted in trying to reason with her.

"Is it worth it, just for blue hair?"

"Ask her, not me," snapped Mum, and pulled me after the pushchair so sharply she practically wrenched my arm out of its socket.

So I asked her. I asked Gran the very next time that I bumped into her, picking her way around the muddy patch of the shortcut across the recreation ground.

I spread my hands out in what the author of my *Best Bible Stories* always refers to as a "beseeching fashion."

"Is it worth it, Gran, just for blue hair?" I cried.

What Gran said was almost as rude as what Mum said. I shan't repeat that, either. But I confess to being a little shocked. She is my granny, after all.

I left the two of them to it, after that. I knew the problem couldn't last forever because Crusher had told me Mum's blue was the sort that washed out. So I concentrated my efforts on cheering Crummy Dummy, who didn't know that. I made Crusher fix up her baby-bouncer. It's not been right since Mum took off half the chain links to wear to a dance. And I made the hole in her bottle a whole lot bigger. She's been sucking and blowing like a smoker when the lift's broken, trying to get the milk out, poor thing. And I cut the feet off the ends of her striped babygrow suit. I reckon her toes were getting all squashed up.

And I waited. But Gran never came, and Mum never even went next door to phone her. It was nearly a week.

"What a stubborn pair of bats!" was the only remark Crusher made about the whole sorry business.

And then, just as I was despairing, there came the night of the gale.

What a night that was! The rain beat down, lashing against the window panes till every dream turned into a nightmare. It was still dark at breakfast time. Storm water was seeping under the kitchen door, and running over the lino in rivulets. The wind was so fierce it would have had Crummy Dummy's bonnet off in a flash, if I hadn't insisted Mum leave her with old Mrs. Pitopoulos next door, instead of dragging her out in the stroller.

"I don't *need* chumming to school," I told

Mum when she was still scouring the cupboards hopelessly for her scarlet plastic bonsun's helmet at seven minutes to nine. "You don't *have* to come with me."

"You don't *have* to go," she countered irritably.

"I do," I insisted. "It's a school day, isn't it? I'm not sick, or injured, am I?"

"Don't push your luck, Minna," she said, climbing into her galoshes and scowling.

So we set off to school through the gale.

You've never seen anything like it. The street was absolutely clean! All of the litter had been washed away—even the tatty old cardboard boxes outside number twelve, and those great lengths of stair carpet on the corner that the garbage men have refused for four whole weeks to shove into their mechanical chewer.

The main road was amazing, too. Cars were crawling along with their drivers hunched forward and peering through little arcs on the windscreens. The tires hurled wide sheets of filthy gutter water up in our faces. Mum spat and cursed. Her galoshes were flooded.

And just at that moment, I noticed Gran. She was staggering out of her cul-de-sac, into the

wind, fighting her umbrella, which looked just as though it were fighting her back.

I squeezed Mum's arm.

"Look," I said, pointing. "Gran! And we're

going the same way."

Mum blinked raindrops off her eyelashes, and looked. Then she shouted to me over the wind:

"I'm not slowing up. Not in this weather. And now I'm this wet, I'm not going back either."

And, with that, she strode on with her head down against the spiteful winds and the rain.

Gran was striding along, almost beside us. She clearly had the same idea. The weather was far too awful to slow up, or take a longer route, or go back home and set off again later. She was going to brazen it out, just like Mum.

The two of them were practically side by side now, each striding along into the wind, and neither of them so much as giving one tiny little sideways peep at the other.

And that was their big mistake! For the oddest thing was happening. The strangest sight! Both of them were changing. It was almost as if the storm were playing its own little private joke on the pair of them.

Mum's hair was changing back to its normal color! First, little streaks started running like tiny bright blue rivers down her cheeks, over her ears, and down the back of her neck. Her hair was gradually returning to mousey brown, the color it was before she went royal blue. The dye was washing out, faster and faster. And the spikes were collapsing. The wind was blowing them flat. Mum didn't notice, but by the time we reached the corner, she looked as clean and neat and tidy as she does in the photo that was taken of her at convent school.

(Gran loves that photo. She keeps it on the mantelpiece at her house in a special fur frame. Mum says it makes her look like a wally, and slams it down on its face whenever we visit. If the frame wasn't fur, she'd have smashed it by now, doing that.)

And Mum wasn't the only one looking different. Gran was changing, too. As she marched into the same fierce wind, her neat little parting was whipped away, and patches of her hair stuck up in clumps, like Crusher's after his football practice. Her hair was wet, too, making the blue look bluer. Gran no longer looked like someone who'd been to the hair-dresser only ten days ago. She looked like some-one who'd been dragged backward through a hedge.

Then, as we reached the school gates, the wind gave one last, amazing flourish. It whipped Gran's hair up into spikes. It whipped a nice neat parting into Mum's straight brown hair. And it whipped the umbrella clean out of Gran's grasp.

Mum reached out and caught the handle automatically, as it flew past. Then, since she couldn't think of anything else to do with it, she turned to Gran to hand it back.

Gran turned to her, to take it.

Both of them stared.

Gran stared at neat, sweet, tidy Mum, looking just like she used to look in her favorite photo on the mantelpiece.

Mum stared at punky, spiky, blue Gran, looking a bit like Crusher Maggot on a bad morning.

Tears came to Gran's eyes first.

"Look at you! You look *lovely*!" she cried, and reached out to give Mum one of her giant hugs.

"And you!" Mum squealed with pleasure, hugging her back. "You look smashing, just smashing!"

"What a wonderful surprise!"

"Oh, you are too! Really!"

I sighed, and shook my head. Then the school bell rang. I walked away, and neither of them even noticed. They were far too busy praising one another for their beautiful hairstyles.

It's a good job there are no mirrors hanging

on our school wall, I reckoned. But you never know . . . . In my experience, most of their silly squabbles get sorted out in time, if you just ignore them.

STRONG BUT QUIRKY

Irwin Shapiro

The morning Davy Crockett was born Davy's Pa came busting out of his cabin in Tennessee alongside the Nolachucky River. He fired three shots into the air, gave a whoop, and said, "I've got me a son. His name is Davy Crockett, and he'll be the greatest hunter in all creation."

When he said that the sun rose up in the sky like a ball of fire. The wind howled riproariously. Thunder boomed, and all the critters and varmints of the forest let out a moan.

Then Davy's Pa went back into the cabin. Little Davy was stretched out in a cradle made of a snapping turtle's shell. There was a pair of elk horns over the top, and over the elk horns water power, and it was rocking away—rockety-whump, rockety-whump.

Now all the Crocketts were big, but Davy was big even for a Crockett. He weighed two hundred pounds, fourteen ounces, and he was as frisky as a wildcat. His Ma and his Aunt Ketinah stood over Davy, trying to get him to sleep.

"Sing somethin' to quiet the boy," said Aunt Ketinah to his Uncle Roarious, who was standing in a corner combing his hair with a rake.

Uncle Roarious opened his mouth and sang a bit of "Over the River to Charley". That is, it was meant for singing. It sounded worse than a nor'easter howling around a country barn at midnight.

"Hmmm," said Uncle Roarious. He reached for a jug and took him a sip of kerosene oil to loosen up his pipes.

Davy was sitting up in his cradle. He kept his peepers on his uncle, watching him pull at the jug.

"I'll have a sip o' the same," said Davy, as loud as you please.

That kerosene jug slipped right out of Uncle Roarious's hand. Davy's Ma and his Aunt Ketinah let out a shriek.

"Why, the little shaver can talk!" said Davy's Pa.

"We-el," said Davy, talking slow and easy-like, "maybe I don't jabber good enough to make a speech in Congress, but I reckon I got the hang of 'er. It's nothin' to Davy Crockett."

"That's mighty big talk, Son," said Davy's Pa.

"It ought to be," said Davy. "It's comin' from a big man."

And with that he leaped out of his cradle, kicked his heels together, and crowed like a rooster. He flapped his arms and he bellowed, "I'm Davy Crockett, fresh from the backwoods! I'm half horse, half alligator, with a little touch o' snappin' turtle! I can wade the Mississippi, ride a streak o' lightnin', hug a bear too close for comfort, and whip my weight in wildcats! I can outeat, outsleep, outfight, outshoot, outrun, outjump, and outsquat any man in these here United States! And I will!"

Aunt Ketinah eyed him as if he was a little bit of a mosquito making a buzz.

"That'll be enough o' your sass," said she, kind of sharplike. "Now get back into your cradle and behave."

"Yes, ma'am," said Davy. He was always polite to the ladies.

"No such thing!" said Uncle Roarious. "Settin' in the cradle won't grow him none! We've got to plant him in the earth and water him with wild buffalo's milk, with boiled corncobs and tobacco leaves mixed in."

"Can't do any harm," said Davy's Ma.

"Might do good," said Davy's Pa.

"Suits me," said Davy. "Let's give 'er a try."

So they took Davy out to Thunder Shower Hill and planted him in the earth. They watered him with wild buffalo's milk, with boiled corncobs and tobacco leaves mixed in. The sun shone on him by day, and the moon beamed down on him by night. The wind cooled him and rain freshened him. And Davy Crockett began to grow proper.

One morning Davy's Pa got up as usual and looked out the window. Instead of the sun shining, it was like a cloudy night with fog and no moon. Davy's Pa had never seen it so dark in all his born days.

"Hurricane's comin' up," he said to Uncle Roarious, who was standing in a corner buttoning up his cast-iron shirt.

"We'd better water Davy before she breaks," said Uncle Roarious.

Davy's Pa and Uncle Roarious each picked

up a barrel of wild buffalo's milk, with boiled corncobs and tobacco leaves mixed in. Davy's Ma and Aunt Ketinah followed along, carrying another barrel between them.

But when they got outside there wasn't a sign of a hurricane. There wasn't any hurricane at all. The sky was blue with little white clouds, and the sun was shining just as pretty. Only reason it was dark was that Davy's shadow was falling over the cabin.

"Davy must have growed some," said Davy's Ma, and they all hurried over to Thunder Shower Hill. Davy was standing on tiptoe with his head poked through a cloud. He was taller than the tallest tree and a sight friskier.

Uncle Roarious let out a yip and Davy leaned down. Davy wiped a bit of cloud out of his eye and said, "I've been lookin' over the country. She's right pretty, and I think I'm goin' to like 'er."

"You'd better," said Aunt Ketinah, kind of snappylike. "She's the only one you've got."

"Yes, ma'am!" roared out Davy. His voice was so loud it started an avalanche at Whang-doodle Knob, thirty miles away. The trees all around flattened out, and Aunt Ketinah, Uncle Roarious, and Davy's Ma and Pa fell over from the force of it.

Davy's Pa picked himself up and shook his head.

"He's too big," he said.

"Oh, I don't know," said Uncle Roarious. "He'll settle some."

"No," said Davy's Pa, "he's too big for a hunter. It wouldn't be fair and square."

"What are we goin' to do?" asked Uncle Roarious.

"Only one thing *to* do," said Davy's Pa. "We've got to uproot him and let him grow down to man-size."

So Davy's Ma and Pa, his Aunt Ketinah, and his Uncle Roarious uprooted Davy. Soon as his feet were free, Davy leaped high into the air. He kicked his heels together, flapped his arms, and he bellowed, "Look out, all you critters and varmints o' the forest. For here comes Davy Crockett, fresh from the backwoods! I'm half horse, half alligator, with a little touch o' snappin' turtle! I can run faster, jump higher, squat lower, dive deeper, stay under water longer, and come up drier than any man in these here United States! Who-o-o-o-o-p!"

Uncle Roarious listened to Davy and he looked at Davy. Then he said, "He's strong, but he's quirky."

Davy's Pa looked at Davy and he listened to Davy.

"He'll do," he said. "He'll do for a Crockett till a better one comes along."

And when Davy's Pa said that, lightning flashed and thunder boomed. The wind howled riproariously, and all the critters and varmints of the forest let out a moan.

WILLIAM'S VERSION

Jan Mark

William and Granny were left to entertain each other for an hour while William's mother went to the clinic.

"Sing to me," said William.

"Granny's too old to sing," said Granny.

"I'll sing to you, then," said William. William only knew one song. He had forgotten the words and the tune, but he sang it several times, anyway.

"Shall we do something else now?" said Granny.

"Tell me a story," said William. "Tell me about the wolf."

"Red Riding Hood?"

"No, not *that* wolf, the other wolf."

"Peter and the wolf?" said Granny.

"Mummy's going to have a baby," said William.

"I know," said Granny.

William looked suspicious.

"How do you know?"

"Well . . . she told me. And it shows, doesn't it?"

"The lady down the road had a baby. It looks like a pig," said William. He counted on his fingers. "Three babies looks like three pigs."

"Ah," said Granny. "Once upon a time there were three little pigs. Their names were—"

"They didn't have names," said William.

"Yes they did. The first pig was called—"

"Pigs don't have names."

"Some do. These pigs had names."

"No they didn't." William slid off Granny's lap and went to open the corner cupboard by the fireplace. Old magazines cascaded out as old magazines do when they have been flung into a cupboard and the door slammed shut. He rooted among them until he found a little book covered with brown paper, climbed into the cupboard, opened the book, closed it and climbed out again. "They didn't have names," he said.

"I didn't know you could read," said Granny, properly impressed.

"C-A-T, wheelbarrow," said William.

"Is that the book Mummy reads to you out of?"

"It's my book," said William.

"But it's the one Mummy reads?"

"If she says please," said William.

"Well, that's Mummy's story, then. My pigs have names."

"They're the wrong pigs." William was not open to negotiation. "I don't want them in this story."

"Can't we have different pigs this time?"

"No. They won't know what to do."

"Once upon a time," said Granny, "there were three little pigs who lived with their mother."

"Their mother was dead," said William.

42

"Oh, I'm sure she wasn't," said Granny.

"She was dead. You make bacon out of dead pigs. She got eaten for breakfast and they threw the rind out for the birds."

"So the three little pigs had to find homes for themselves."

"No." William consulted his book. "They had to build little houses."

"I'm just coming to that."

"You said they had to *find* homes. They didn't *find* them."

"The first little pig walked along for a bit until he met a man with a load of hay."

"It was a lady."

"A lady with a load of hay?"

"NO! It was a lady-pig. You said *he*."

"I thought all the pigs were little boy-pigs," said Granny.

"It says lady-pig here," said William. "It says the lady-pig went for a walk and met a man with a load of hay."

"So the lady-pig," said Granny, "said to the man, 'May I have some of that hay to build a house?' and the man said, 'Yes.' Is that right?"

"Yes," said William. "You know that baby?"

"What baby?"

"The one Mummy's going to have. Will that baby have shoes on when it comes out?"

"I don't think so," said Granny.

"It will have cold feet," said William.

"Oh no," said Granny. "Mummy will wrap it up in a soft shawl, all snug."

"I don't *mind* if it has cold feet," William explained. "Go on about the lady-pig."

"So the little lady-pig took the hay and built a little house. Soon the wolf came along and the wolf said—"

"You didn't tell where the wolf lived."

"I don't know where the wolf lived."

"15 Tennyson Avenue, next to the bomb site," said William.

"I bet it doesn't say that in the book," said Granny, with spirit.

"Yes it does."

"Let me see, then."

William folded himself up with his back to Granny, and pushed the book up under his pullover.

"*I* don't think it says that

44

in the book," said Granny.

"It's in ever so small words," said William.

"So the wolf said, 'Little pig, little pig, let me come in,' and the little pig answered, 'No.' So the wolf said, 'Then I'll huff and I'll puff and I'll blow your house down,' and he huffed and he puffed and he blew the house down, and the little pig ran away."

"He ate the little pig," said William.

"No, no," said Granny. "The little pig ran away."

"He ate the little pig. He ate her in a sandwich."

"All right, he ate the little pig in a sandwich. So the second little pig—"

"You didn't tell about the tricycle."

"What about the tricycle?"

"The wolf got on his tricycle and went to the bread shop to buy some bread. To make the sandwich," William explained, patiently.

"Oh well, the wolf got on his tricycle and went to the bread shop to buy some bread. And he went to the grocer's to buy some butter."

This innovation did not go down well.

"He already had some butter in the cupboard," said William.

"So then the second little pig went for a walk and met a man with a load of wood, and the little pig said to the man, 'May I have some of that wood to build a house?' and the man said, 'Yes.'"

"He didn't say please."

"'Please may I have some of that wood to build a house?'"

"It was sticks."

"Sticks *are* wood."

William took out his book and turned the pages. "That's right," he said.

"Why don't you tell the story?" said Granny.

"I can't remember it," said William.

"You could read it out of your book."

"I've lost it," said William, clutching his pullover. "Look, do you know who this is?" He pulled a green angora scarf from under the sofa.

"No, who is it?" said Granny, glad of the diversion.

"This is Doctor Snake." He made the scarf wriggle across the carpet.

"Why is he a doctor?"

"Because he is all furry," said William. He wrapped the doctor round his neck and sat sucking the loose end.

"Go on about the wolf."

"So the little pig built a house of sticks and along came the wolf—on his tricycle?"

"He came by bus. He didn't have any money for a ticket so he ate up the conductor."

"That wasn't very nice of him," said Granny.

"No," said William. "It wasn't *very* nice."

"And the wolf said, 'Little pig, little pig, let me come in,' and the little pig said, 'No,' and the wolf said, 'Then I'll huff and I'll puff and I'll blow your house down,' so he huffed and he puffed and he blew the house down. And then what did he do?" Granny asked, cautiously.

William was silent.

"Did he eat the second little pig?"

"Yes."

"How did he eat this little pig?" said Granny, prepared for more pig sandwiches or possibly pig on toast.

"With his mouth," said William.

"Now the third little pig went for a walk and met a man with a load of bricks. And the little pig said, '*Please* may I have some of those bricks to build a house?' and the man said, 'Yes.' So the little pig took the bricks and built a house."

"He built it on the bomb site."

47

"Next door to the wolf?" said Granny. "That was very silly of him."

"There wasn't anywhere else," said William. "All the roads were full up."

"The wolf didn't have to come by bus or tricycle this time, then, did he?" said Granny, grown cunning.

"Yes." William took out the book and peered in, secretively. "He was playing in the cemetery. He had to get another bus."

"And did he eat the conductor this time?"

"No. A nice man gave him some money, so he bought a ticket."

"I'm glad to hear it," said Granny.

"He ate the nice man," said William.

"So the wolf got off the bus and went up to the little pig's house, and he said, 'Little pig, little pig, let me come in,' and the little pig said, 'No,' and then the wolf said, 'I'll huff and I'll puff and I'll blow your house down,' and he huffed and he puffed and he huffed and he puffed but he couldn't blow the house down because it was made of bricks."

"He couldn't blow it

48

down," said William, "because it was stuck to the ground."

"Well, anyway, the wolf got very cross then, and he climbed on the roof and shouted down the chimney, 'I'm coming to get you!' but the little pig just laughed and put a big saucepan of water on the fire."

"He put it on the gas stove."

"He put it on the *fire*," said Granny, speaking very rapidly, "and the wolf fell down the chimney and into the pan of water and was boiled and the little pig ate him for supper."

William threw himself full length on the carpet and screamed.

"He didn't! He didn't! *He didn't!* He didn't eat the wolf."

Granny picked him up, all stiff and kicking, and sat him on her lap.

"Did I get it wrong again, love? Don't cry. Tell me what really happened."

William wept, and wiped his nose on Doctor Snake.

"The little pig put the saucepan on the gas stove and the wolf got down the chimney and put the little pig in the saucepan and boiled him. He had him for tea, with chips," said William.

"Oh," said Granny. "I've got it all wrong, haven't I? Can I see the book, then I shall know, next time."

William took the book from under his pullover. Granny opened it and read, *First Aid for Beginners: a Practical Handbook*.

"I see," said Granny. "I don't think I can read this. I left my glasses at home. You tell Gran how it ends."

William turned to the last page which showed a prostrate man with his leg in a splint; *compound fracture of the femur*.

"Then the wolf washed up and got on his tricycle and went to see his Granny, and his Granny opened the door and said, 'Hello, William.'"

"I thought it was the wolf."

"It was. It was the wolf. His name was William Wolf," said William.

"What a nice story," said Granny. "You tell it much better than I do."

"I can see up your nose," said William. "It's all whiskery."

ANANCY
AND TIGER

A Caribbean Tale
retold by Andrew Matthews

Tiger was a friend of Anancy, the spider man, and you can't imagine two friends more different. Tiger was big and handsome with bulging muscles and a voice that boomed like thunder. Anancy was thin and weak. He limped when he walked and he lisped when he talked. His voice sounded as dry and whispery as leaves in the wind.

"Anancy was small, but he was clever. He played tricks on people and the tricks made Tiger laugh. Tiger never dreamed that Anancy would dare trick him, but he did and this is how it happened.

One hot day, Anancy and Tiger went to swim in the river. Tiger took his dinner with him, in a tin with a handle. As they walked along together, Anancy said, "My, my, my!

51

Something smells good!"

"That's my dinner," said Tiger. "It's fish stew with dumplings—my favorite!"

It was Anancy's favorite too, and his mouth watered at the thought of it. He wanted the stew, but to get it he would have to come up with a good trick. His mind began to spin webs of plans.

"Let's go somewhere new to swim today, Tiger!" he said. "I know a pool where the river runs deep."

"All right," said Tiger. "But you're not a very good swimmer, Anancy. Are you sure you can manage in deep water?"

"I'll be all right," said Anancy. "I know you'll help me if I get into trouble, because we're such good friends. After all, we share everything, don't we?"

"Everything except my dinner," said Tiger. "I like fish stew with dumplings so much that I don't want to share it with anyone."

It was noon when they reached the pool and the sun was baking hot.

"You go first, Tiger," said Anancy. "See how deep the water really is."

Tiger was longing to swim in the cool river. He put his tin of stew on an old stump where he could keep an eye on it, then he plunged into the pool with a great splash.

"What a wonderful dive!" exclaimed Anancy. "You're a very good swimmer, Tiger, but I wonder if you're good enough to swim right down to the bottom of the pool?"

"Of course I am!" Tiger said boastfully. "Just watch this!"

Tiger took a deep breath and disappeared under the water.

Anancy ran over to the stump and emptied Tiger's tin onto a big leaf, which he hid behind a tree.

Tiger came up from the bottom of the river with a whoosh. He looked around and saw that his tin was just where he had left it.

"Anancy?" Tiger shouted. "Are you coming swimming or not?"

"In a minute, Tiger, old friend," said Anancy. "I'll just have a snooze in the shade of this tree and then I'll join you."

Tiger carried on splashing and diving and Anancy went behind the tree. He gobbled down every scrap of Tiger's fish stew and licked the leaf until not even a spot of gravy was left. Just as he finished, Anancy heard Tiger calling.

"Are you still snoozing, Anancy, you lazy good-for-nothing? I'll have to come and get you and throw you in!"

Anancy was worried—if Tiger came out of the water, he would see that the stew tin was empty. He hurried down to the edge of the pool and began to moan and groan.

"What's the matter?" asked Tiger.

"Ooh, I feel ill!" whimpered Anancy. "I must go home and lie down! I can't go swimming today."

"If you're so ill, I'd better come with you," said Tiger.

"No, no!" said Anancy. "Don't let me spoil

your swim! You stay in the water and have a good time. Don't worry about me."

Anancy limped off down the path until he came to a bend. He turned and waved at Tiger, who waved back. Anancy turned the corner and then went scuttling off as fast as his little legs could carry him.

Before long he reached Monkey Village. Anancy changed his scuttle to a shuffling dance and he went down the main street singing quietly. The monkeys were all out on their verandas, and when Anancy appeared they cocked their heads to one side to try and catch when he was singing.

"Hey, Anancy, what's that song?" one of the monkeys asked.

"It's a new song I heard the other day," Anancy said slyly. "Would you like me to teach it to you?"

The monkeys liked nothing better than singing and dancing and they eagerly crowded round Anancy.

"The words go like this," Anancy told them.

"Call me a thief,
Call me a sinner
But today I ate old Tiger's dinner."

"That's a great song!" chattered the monkeys. "Hey, Anancy, we'll sing it at the dance tonight.

Why don't you come along?"

"I'll be there," said Anancy.

Anancy hid in a tree near Monkey Village and waited for evening. As soon as the sun went down, the monkeys began to drink palm wine and before long they were dancing in the village street, singing the new song at the tops of their voices. Anancy climbed down and hurried off to his own village to find Tiger.

Tiger was in a terrible rage. All afternoon he'd been shouting at the other animals, accusing them of stealing his dinner.

"Ah, Anancy!" Tiger snarled when he saw the spider approaching. "I want a word with you about that stew of mine!"

"And I want a word with you," said Anancy. "Come with me, I want you to hear something."

"What?" said Tiger.

"A new song they're singing down in Monkey Village," said Anancy.

"Look here!" spluttered Tiger, "I've been robbed of my dinner and I want to find out who did it! I haven't got time for songs!"

"If you want to find out what happened to your stew, you'd better come with me," said Anancy.

Growling and grumbling, Tiger followed Anancy down the road. They stopped just outside Monkey Village.

"Hear that?" said Anancy.

"I hear a lot of monkeys singing— and a terrible sound it is too," said Tiger.

"Get closer so you can hear the words of the song!" said Anancy.

Tiger walked a little farther down the road and listened carefully. He heard the monkeys singing,

"Call me a thief,
Call me a sinner,
But today I ate old Tiger's dinner!"

"Oh, so you did, did you!" shouted Tiger. He ran down the main street of Monkey Village, roaring like a hurricane and flashing his teeth.

The monkeys scattered screeching into the jungle, wondering what had made Tiger so angry with them.

As for Anancy, he went to hide. He knew that sooner or later Tiger would find out who had taught the monkeys the song and he wanted to be far away when it happened. Anancy ran along the road, chuckling and singing to himself.

"Call me a thief,
Call me a sinner
But today I ate old Tiger's dinner.
Tiger was splashing in a deep, deep pool,
He's a strong, strong swimmer,
But a big, big fool!"

THE LIBRARIAN
AND
THE ROBBERS

Margaret Mahy

One day Serena Laburnum, the beautiful librarian, was carried off by wicked robbers. She had just gone for a walk in the woods at the edge of the town, when the robbers came charging at her and carried her off.

"Why are you kidnapping me?" she asked coldly. "I have no wealthy friends or relatives. Indeed I am an orphan with no real home but the library."

"That's just it," said the Robber Chief. "The City Council will pay richly to have you restored. After all, everyone knows that the library does not work properly without you."

This was especially true because Miss Laburnum had the library keys.

"I think I ought to warn you," she said, "that I spent the weekend with a friend of mine who

59

has four little boys. Everyone in the house had the dread disease of Raging Measles."

"That's all right!" said the Robber Chief, sneering a bit. "I've had them."

"But I haven't!" said the robber at his elbow, and the other robbers looked at Miss Laburnum uneasily. None of them had had the dread disease of Raging Measles.

As soon as the robbers' ransom note was received by the City Council, there was a lot of discussion. Everyone was anxious that things should be done in the right way.

"What is it when our librarian is kidnapped?" asked a councillor. "Is it staff expenditure or does it come out of the cultural fund?"

"The Cultural Committee meets in a fortnight," said the Mayor. "I propose we let them make a decision on this."

But long before that, all the robbers (except the Robber Chief) had Raging Measles.

First of all they became very irritable and had red sniffy noses.

I *think* a hot bath brings out the rash," said Miss Laburnum doubtfully. "Oh, if only I were in my library I would be able to look up measles in my *Dictionary of Efficient and Efficacious Home Nursing.*"

The Robber Chief looked gloomily at his gang.

"Are you sure it's measles?" he said. "That's a very undignified complaint for a robber to suffer from. There are few people who are improved by spots, but for robbers they are disastrous. Would you take a spotty robber seriously?"

"It is no part of a librarian's duty to take any robber seriously, spotty or otherwise," said Miss

Laburnum haughtily. "And, anyhow, there must be no robbing until they have got over the Raging Measles. They are in quarantine. After all you don't want to be blamed for spreading measles everywhere, do you?"

The Robber Chief groaned.

"If you will allow me," said Miss Laburnum, "I will go back to my library and borrow *The Dictionary of Efficient and Efficacious Home Nursing*. With the help of that invaluable book I shall try to alleviate the sufferings of your fellows. Of course I shall only be able to take it out for a week. It is a special reference book, you see."

The groaning of his fellows suffering from Raging Measles was more than the Robber Chief could stand.

"All right," he said. "You can go and get that

book, and we'll call off the kidnapping for the present. Just a temporary measure."

In a short time Miss Laburnum was back with several books.

"A hot bath to bring out the rash!" she announced reading clearly and carefully. "Then you must have the cave darkened, and you mustn't read or play cards. You have to be careful of your eyes when you have measles."

The robbers found it very dull, lying in a darkened cave. Miss Laburnum took their temperatures and asked them if their ears hurt.

"It's very important that you keep warm," she told them, pulling blankets up to their robberish beards, and tucking them in so tightly that they could not toss or turn. "But to make the time go quickly I will read to you. Now, what have you read already?"

These robbers had not read a thing. They were almost illiterate. "Very well," said Miss Laburnum, "we shall start with Peter Rabbit and work our way up from there."

Never in all their lives had those robbers been read to. In spite of the fever induced by Raging Measles they listened intently and asked for more. The Robber Chief listened too, though Miss Laburnum had given him the task of making nourishing broth for the invalids.

"Tell us more about that Brer Rabbit!" was the fretful cry of the infectious villains. "Read to us about Alice in Wonderland."

Robin Hood made them uneasy. He was a robber, as they were, but full of noble thoughts such as giving to the poor. These robbers had not planned on giving to the poor, but only on keeping for themselves.

After a few days the spots began to disappear, and the robbers began to get hungry. Miss Laburnum dipped into her *Dictionary of Efficient and Efficacious Home Nursing*, and found some tempting recipes for convalescents. She wrote them out for the Robber Chief. Having given up the idea of kidnapping Miss Laburnum, the Robber Chief now had the idea of kidnapping the book, but Miss Laburnum wouldn't let him have it.

"It is used by a lot of people who belong to the library," she said. "But, of course, if you want to check up on anything later you may always come to the library and consult it."

Shortly after this the robbers were quite recovered and Miss Laburnum, with her keys, went back to town. It seemed that robbers were a thing of the past. *The Dictionary of Efficient and Efficacious Home Nursing* was restored to the library shelves. The library was opened once more to the hordes who had been starved of literature during the days of Miss Laburnum's kidnapping.

Yet, about three weeks after all these dramatic events, there was more robber trouble!

Into the library, in broad daylight, burst none other than the Robber Chief.

"Save me!" he cried. "A policeman is after me."

Miss Laburnum gave him a cool look.

"You had better give me your full name," she said. "Quickly!"

The Robber Chief sprang back, an expression of horror showing through his black tangled beard.

"No, no!" he cried, "anything but that!"

"Quickly," repeated Miss Laburnum, "or I won't have time to help you."

The Robber Chief leaned across the desk

and whispered his name to her . . . "Salvation Loveday."

Miss Laburnum could not help smiling a little bit. It certainly went very strangely with those wiry whiskers.

"They used to call me Sally at school," cried the unhappy robber. "It's that name that has driven me to a life of crime. But hide me, dear Miss Laburnum, or I shall be caught."

Miss Laburnum stamped him with a number, as if he was a library book, and put him into a bookshelf with a lot of books whose authors had surnames beginning with "L." He was in strict alphabetical order. Alphabetical order is a habit with librarians.

The policeman who had been chasing the Robber Chief burst into the library. He was a good runner, but he had fallen over a little boy on a tricycle, and this had slowed him down.

"Miss Laburnum," said the policeman, "I have just had occasion to pursue a notable Robber Chief into your library. I can see him there in the bookshelves among the Ls. May I take him out please?"

"Certainly!" said Miss Laburnum pleasantly. "Do you have your library membership card?"

The policeman's face fell.

"Oh, dear," he said, "No . . . I'm afraid it's at home marking the place in my *Policeman's Robber-Catching Compendium*."

Miss Laburnum gave a polite smile.

"I'm afraid you can't withdraw anything without your membership card," she said. "That Robber Chief is Library Property."

The policeman nodded slowly. He knew it was true: you weren't allowed to take anything out of the library without your library card. This was a strict library rule. "I'll just tear home and get it," he said. "I don't live very far away."

"Do that," said Miss Laburnum pleasantly.

The policeman's strong police boots rang out as he hurried from the library.

Miss Laburnum went to the "L" shelf and took down the Robber Chief. "Now, what are you doing *here*?" she said severely. However, the Robber Chief was not fooled—she was really very pleased to see him.

67

"Well," he replied, "the fact is, Miss Laburnum, my men are restless. Ever since you read them those stories, they've been discontented in the evening. We used to sit around our campfire singing rumbustical songs and indulging in rough humor, but they've lost their taste for it. They're wanting more *Brer Rabbit*, more *Treasure Island*, and more stories of kings and clowns. Today I was coming to join the library and take some books out for them. What shall I do? I daren't go back without books, and yet that policeman may return. And won't he be very angry with you when he finds I'm gone?"

"That will be taken care of," said Miss Laburnum, smiling to herself. "What is your number? Ah, yes. Well, when the policeman returns, I will tell him someone else has taken you out, and it will be true, for you are now issued to me."

The Robber Chief gave Miss Laburnum a very speaking look.

"And now," said Miss Laburnum cheerfully, "you must join the library yourself and take out some books for your poor robbers."

"If I am a member of the library myself, perhaps I could take you out," said the Robber Chief with robberish boldness. Miss Laburnum quickly changed the subject, but she blushed as she did so.

She sent the Robber Chief off with some splendid story books.

He had only just gone when the policeman came back.

"Now," said the policeman, producing his membership card, "I'd like to take out that Robber Chief, if I may."

He looked so expectant it seemed a pity to disappoint him. Miss Laburnum glanced toward the Ls.

"Oh," she said, "I'm afraid he has already been taken out by someone else. You should have reserved him."

The policeman stared at the shelf very hard. Then he stared at Miss Laburnum.

"May I put my name down for him?" he asked after a moment.

"Certainly," said Miss Laburnum, "though I ought to warn you that you may have a long wait ahead of you. There could be a long waiting list."

After this the Robber Chief came sneaking into town regularly to change books. It was dangerous, but he thought it was worth it.

As the robbers read more and more, their culture and philosophy deepened, until they were the most cultural and philosophic band of robbers one could wish to encounter. As for Miss Laburnum, there is no doubt that she was aiding and abetting robbers; not very good behavior in a librarian, but she had her reasons.

Then came the day of the terrible earthquake. Chimneys fell down all over town. Every building creaked and rattled. Out in the forest the robbers felt it and stood aghast as trees swayed and pinecones came tumbling around them like hailstones. At last the ground was still again. The Robber Chief went pale.

"The library!" he called. "What will have happened to Miss Laburnum and the books?"

Every other robber turned pale too. You never saw such a lot of palefaced robbers at one and the same time.

"Quickly!" they shouted. "To the rescue! Rescue Miss Laburnum. Save the books."

Shouting such words as these they all ran down the road out of the forest and into town.

The policeman saw them, but when he heard their heroic cry he decided to help them first and arrest them afterward.

"Save Miss Laburnum!" he shouted. "Rescue the books."

What a terrible scene in the library! Pictures had fallen from the walls and the flowers were upset. Boxes of stamps were overturned and mixed up all over floor. Books had fallen from their shelves like autumn leaves from their trees, and lay all over the floor in helpless confusion.

There was no sign of Miss Laburnum that anyone could see.

Actually Miss Laburnum had been shelving books in the old store—the shelves where they put all the battered old books—when the earthquake came. Ancient, musty encyclopedias showered down upon her. When the earthquake was over she was still alive, but so covered in books that she could not move.

"Pulverized by literature," thought Miss Laburnum. "The ideal way for a librarian to die."

She did not feel very pleased about it, but there was nothing she could do to save herself. Then she heard a heroic cry!

"Serena, Serena Laburnum!" a voice was shouting. Someone was pulling books off her. It was the Robber Chief.

"Salvation is a very good name for you," said Miss Laburnum faintly.

Tenderly he lifted her to her feet and dusted her down.

"I came as soon as I could," he said. "Oh, Miss Laburnum, this may not be the best time to ask you, but as I am giving up a life of crime and becoming respectable, will you marry me? You need someone to lift the books off you, and generally rescue you from time to time. It would make things so much simpler if you would marry me."

"Of course I will," said Miss Laburnum simply. "After all, I did take you out with my library membership card; I must have secretly admired you for a long time."

Out in the main room of the library there was great activity. Robbers and councillors, working together like brothers, were sorting the mixed-up stamps, filing the spilled cards, reshelving the fallen books. The policeman was hanging up some of the pictures. They all cheered when the Robber Chief appeared with Miss Laburnum, bruised but still beautiful.

"Ahem," said the Robber Chief. "I am the happiest man alive. Miss Laburnum has promised to marry me."

A great cheer went up from everyone.

"On one condition," said Miss Laburnum. "That all you robbers give up being robbers and become librarians instead. You weren't very good at being robbers, but I think as librarians you might be excellent. I have come to feel very proud of you all."

The robbers were struck to breathless silence. Never when they were mere inefficient robbers in the forest had they dreamed of such praise. Greatly moved by these sentiments they then and there swore that they would cease to be villains and become librarians instead.

It was all very exciting. Even the policeman wept with joy.

So, ever after, that particular library was remarkably well run. With all the extra librarians they suddenly had, the Council was able to open a children's library with story readings and adventure plays every day. The robber librarians had become very good at such things practicing around their campfires in the forest.

Miss Laburnum, or Mrs. Loveday as she soon became, sometimes suspected that the children's library in their town was—well—a little wilder, a little more humorous, than many other fine libraries she had seen, but she did not care. She did not mind that the robber librarians all wore wiry black whiskers still, nor that they took down all the notices saying "Silence" and "No talking in the library."

Perhaps she herself was more of a robber at heart than anyone ever suspected . . . except, of course, Robber-Chief-and-First-Library-Assistant Salvation Loveday, and he did not tell anyone.

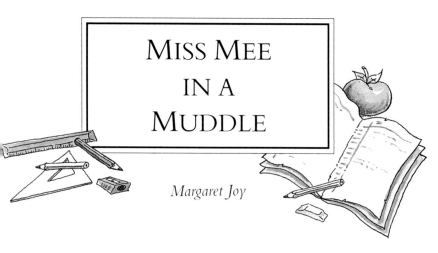

MISS MEE
IN A
MUDDLE

Margaret Joy

In Miss Mee's class were two girls who weren't like any others in the school. They both had brown eyes. They both had long brown hair tied back in pigtails. They each had a dimple in their chins. They each had rosy cheeks. They both sucked their thumbs when they got tired. Their voices even sounded the same when they talked.

They lived in the same house with the same mom and dad and the same little brother. They had their birthday on the same day, and they even came to school wearing clothes that looked exactly the same. Only one thing was different about them: they each had a different name. One was called Rosemary, the other was called Barbara.

The children in Miss Mee's class stared on

75

the day that Rosemary and Barbara first started school. They each wore a red dress and white socks and red sandals, and they each had red ribbons in their hair.

"They're the same," said little Larry.

"They're twins," said Pete.

Rosemary and Barbara soon got used to coming to school, and they made lots of friends. But they still always played together and even cried if Miss Mee asked Rosemary to sit at one table and Barbara to sit at another.

The other children in the class soon knew which twin was Rosemary and which twin was Barbara. But Miss Mee didn't. Sometimes she would say:

"What a lovely painting, Rosemary—or is it Barbara?"

Or she would say:

"Put your puzzle away now, Barbara—or are you Rosemary?"

The other children always laughed and told Miss Mee which twin was which, but Miss Mee still went on getting muddled up.

Then one day she had a bright idea. She bought two badges and she wrote "Barbara" on one and "Rosemary" on the other. She asked the twins to put them on.

"There!" said Miss Mee, very pleased at her bright idea. "Now I shan't make any more mistakes. The twin with the Barbara badge is Barbara and the twin with the Rosemary badge is Rosemary. Now we'll know!"

For a few days this worked very well and Miss Mee made no mistakes. But one afternoon when Barbara, Rosemary and Ian were playing in the play-house, Ian suddenly had an idea. He whispered to the twins, and they giggled. They swapped over badges and giggled again. Then they went with Ian to show Miss Mee.

"We've done something you can't guess," said Rosemary.

"What's that then, Barbara?" asked Miss Mee, looking at her badge to see who she was.

"We've played a trick on you," said Barbara.

"What sort of a trick, Rosemary?" asked Miss Mee, looking at her badge to see who she was.

"They're not Barbara and Rosemary," said Ian. "They're Rosemary and Barbara!"

"We've swapped badges," said the twins together, and giggled.

"Oh dear, now I'm in a muddle again," said Miss Mee.

After school she told the twins' mother what they had done. Their mother laughed.

"I'll give them different-colored ribbons for their hair tomorrow," she said. "Red for Rosemary, blue for Barbara—then you'll know which is which."

Miss Mee thought that was a wonderful idea. Next morning she asked the twins to stand in front of the class. She asked the twin with the red ribbons who she was. Everybody answered for her:

"Rosemary, that's Rosemary!"

"So *you* must be Barbara," said Miss Mee to the little girl with blue ribbons. "R for Rosemary and red; B for Barbara and blue. I'll remember that and never get you muddled up again."

This worked very well for quite a long time.

"Good night, Rosemary; good night, Barbara," called Miss Mee one Friday evening, and she knew she'd got it right.

On Monday morning the twins were a few minutes late.

"Where can they be?" asked Miss Mee. Then the door opened and everyone looked up and said, "Oooh! Look at the twins! Wow—look at them."

There stood the twins in brown shoes and socks, gray skirts and blue blouses—with shining, *short* hair. And no ribbons.

"We had it cut," said one twin.

"We went to the hairdresser's," said the other twin.

"I think it's lovely, Rosemary—or is it Barbara?" said Miss Mee. "Yes, it really suits you, Barbara—or are you Rosemary?"

All the other children laughed and shouted:

"*That* one's Rosemary and *that* one's Barbara!"

But Miss Mee still didn't know which was which or who was who—and she's still trying to sort them out.

THE NIGHT THING

Michael Rosen

"I don't think Horrible Baby knows how to do the Night Thing," said Fat Foot.

"No, I don't think it does," said Slob Head. "I think it's time we took it out at nights instead of leaving it behind with Bone Bum."

"Yeah," said Freckle Belly, "let's all go out TONIGHT!"

"Yes," said Bone Bum, "and I can teach it the Night Thing."

"All right, all right, all right," said Slob Head. "Don't all talk at once!"

"Right," said Fat Foot, "let's get ready. Tonight we teach Horrible Baby how to get into people's dreams."

"Yeah," said Freckle Belly, "the Night Thing, HEE HEE HEE HUFFLE!"

So Slob Head went off and practiced a few

horrible faces in the mirror. It squeezed its ears into its nose. It screwed its cheeks into little balls and made them pop out one at a time.

Fat Foot went off to read a book on how to change color. It looked very difficult. It seemed to be something to do with eating traffic lights.

Freckle Belly was gargling with dishwashing liquid. It was going all frothy around its mouth and up its nose.

Bone Bum was practicing jumping out from behind walls and roaring:

"RAH CAMMUSSKLE SHMOO GARUFF!!!"

Horrible Baby was sleeping in its crib after a long hard day at the nursery throwing toys at the wall.

At about midnight, Slob Head called out, "Time to go out. Get Horrible Baby and let's GO!!"

So Freckle Belly woke up Horrible Baby. It stood on the end of Horrible Baby's crib and jumped on Horrible Baby's head.

That woke up Horrible Baby.

"Oooh, I like that !" said Horrible Baby.

And then all five Horribles went off into the night.

Soon they got into town and started looking for houses where little boys and girls were asleep. It wasn't long before they found a house full of boys and girls, and they stopped and stood outside the door.

"Now listen," whispered Slob Head to Horrible Baby. "Any moment now, you'll see a dream come floating out of that window up there. That's where there's someone sleeping. As soon as that dream comes out, one of us is going to jump on it and ride it back into the room, back into that person's sleep. Watch."

But Horrible Baby wasn't very interested. Horrible Baby was hungry. "Want a cake," said Horrible Baby. "Want a cake, want a cake, want a cake!!"

"Shhhh!" said Fat Foot. "You'll wake the people up and we won't be able to get into their dreams."

"CAKE! CAKE! CAKE!" said Horrible Baby.

Just at that moment, a dream floated out of a window above their heads. It was a reddy-pink color and had a cow in it. The cow was dancing up and down saying, "I'm a dog, I'm a dog, I'm a dog."

Horrible Baby stopped shouting for cake and stared at the dancing cow.

"Now," said Slob Head, "this is where we come in. Who's going to try this one?"

"Me," said Freckle Belly.

"Me," said Bone Bum.

"Well, I'll tell you what," said Slob Head. "You can both go, seeing as you love doing the Night Thing, and you can take Horrible Baby with you."

"Want a cake! CAKE CAKE CAKE!!!" said Horrible Baby.

"Look," said Slob Head, "we haven't brought a cake with us, so you can't have one, OK?"

"Come on," said Bone Bum, "the dream's going."

So Bone Bum and Freckle Belly grabbed Horrible Baby and leaped up into the air, onto the dream. Then, very slowly, they steered it back through the window and into the person's sleep.

The person was Mr. Sugarpants, a man who lived with his wife and ten children, five boys and five girls. They were the cleanest, loveliest, most beautiful children in the whole world because every day Mr. and Mrs. Sugarpants cleaned and polished them. The children never got dirty because they were never allowed to play out. They were never rude because they weren't allowed to speak.

Well, that's not completely true because they were allowed to say "please" and "thank you." Yes, they were the most perfect children ever, but for one thing—they all, secretly, when no one was looking, picked their noses. Hiding away somewhere, under the bed, or in the dark of night, they all picked their noses.

Mr. and Mrs. Sugarpants didn't know about this, though Mr. Sugarpants was just beginning to

think something very nasty was going on. Once, he was sure he saw Dolly Sugarpants with her finger just on its way to her nose.

Sometimes he used to creep around the house with a telescope and a big stick. He promised himself that if ever he found one of the little Sugarpants getting up to anything he would hit them with his big stick. (Only so as to make sure that they stayed being the cleanest, loveliest, most beautiful children in the world.)

Well, it was Mr. Sugarpants's dream that the Horribles were riding on. Bone Bum and Freckle Belly started wriggling around. Freckle Belly started frothing at the mouth. Bone Bum jumped out from behind the dancing cow.

Mr. Sugarpants started frowning in his sleep, then he started shaking and moaning. There was no question of it; he was getting really scared of Bone Bum and Freckle Belly doing the Night Thing in his sleep.

Just then, Horrible Baby called out, "Want a cake, CAKE, CAKE, CAKE!!"

In an instant, the dream disappeared. The dancing cow vanished and the Horribles were left standing in Mr. Sugarpants's room. But worse than that, Horrible Baby had woken up Mr. Sugarpants and there, by the side of the bed, was THE BIG STICK.

Freckle Belly and Bone Bum began to get frightened. This had never happened to them before. What would Mr. Sugarpants do to them? They saw him open his eyes in the dark, and begin to feel for the light by the side of his bed.

Horrible Baby called out, "Want a cake, want a cake, want a cake!"

"Shhhhhh," said Freckle Belly, but its mouth was all so frothy that it came out as, "SHPLUSHLE, FLUSHLE, SPLISH PISH!!!!"

Mr. Sugarpants thought it was some of his children, so he called out, "Go back to bed, children. Remember, no speaking indoors."

"Want a cake!" said Horrible Baby.

"How dare you?" said Mr. Sugarpants. "First you wake me up and then you don't say please."

Mrs. Sugarpants started waking up, ". . . time for a wash children . . . don't forget to wash between your toes . . . polish your shoes . . ."

With all this going on, there was nothing else that Freckle Belly, Bone Bum, and Horrible Baby could do but creep out of the room and make their way downstairs.

Meanwhile, outside, Slob Head and Fat Foot were getting worried.

"Oh no," said Slob Head. "What if the person in there swallowed their dream? And then . . . oh no . . . what if they swallowed Freckle Belly, Bone Bum, and Horrible Baby? We might never see them again. Oh dear!"

"I'm going in," said Fat Foot.

"Me too," said Slob Head and the pair of them slithered in under the front door.

Just as they got in, who should be coming down the stairs but Freckle Belly, Bone Bum, and Horrible Baby? The trouble was, Slob Head and Fat Foot didn't know who it was. And, even worse, Freckle Belly, Bone Bum, and Horrible Baby didn't know it was Slob Head and Fat Foot coming in. It was very, very dark, and suddenly all five bumped into each other with a great big

CRUMP!!!!!

They shouted out:

"SHLOCK MECKDUCK!!! OOFDRECK CRUMF!!!!! DISH! DISH!! DISH!!! UCKLE-BERRY CUSS!!!!!!!!"

And then came the awful wailing, "WANT A CAKE! WANT A CAKE! WANT A CAKE!"

Slob Head grabbed Fat Foot; Freckle Belly grabbed Bone Bum; Bone Bum grabbed

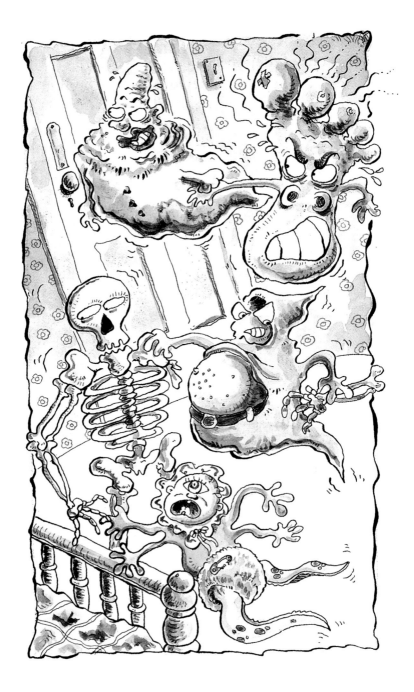

Horrible Baby, and they all dashed for the door, scared out of their lives.

But no one had bothered to open the door. They all landed up in a great heap pushing and squashing and squeezing against the door.

Suddenly the door burst open and the Horribles fell out into the night going, "EEEEEEEPHLE! IMF! SSSSSSSSSSSH-LUMP!!!"

Then, in a great mad rush, they all dashed home as fast as they could go and without another word or noise they jumped into bed and fell asleep.

That night Slob Head dreamed that it was in a box with the lid closed and it was all dark and suddenly Horrible Baby opened the lid of the box and dropped a great big cake right on Slob Head's head.

Fat Foot dreamed that it was looking and looking for something it had lost, and it was very sad; and then suddenly, just as it was about to give up, Horrible Baby appeared and said, "You will never find what you were looking for. It was a cake and I've eaten it."

Freckle Belly dreamed that it was tied to a door and every time someone came and opened the door Freckle Belly's head banged against the wall.

Until, one day, Horrible Baby came along

and said, "You will have to stay here forever and ever banging your head all because you wouldn't give me a cake."

Bone Bum dreamed that it was asleep but then it woke in its dream and found out that it wasn't in its own bed and Horrible Baby was standing over it saying, "I've come to put you in my cake and then I'm going to eat you."

Horrible Baby dreamed of cake.

In the morning Slob Head called the Horribles together and said, "We will not be teaching Horrible Baby how to get into people's dreams again for a long, long time. No more of the Night Thing, OK?"

And all the Horribles nodded.

BUT YOU PROMISED YOU WOULDN'T TELL

Bel Mooney

Dad was going to be in charge. It happened a lot nowadays, because Kitty's Mum's new job meant that sometimes she had to work on Saturdays. Once they got used to it, Kitty and Daniel didn't mind. They always had fun with Dad.

This Saturday morning, Mum was in a bossy mood. "There's plenty of salad in the fridge for lunch," she said, "and I want you to eat it up."

The children groaned.

"Rabbit food," said Daniel.

"I don't want to eat silly, slimy salad," said Kitty.

"Can't we have something else?" they moaned.

But Mum had become very keen on really healthy eating and insisted, "It's *good* for you all

91

—but if you want something hot to go with it, Dad can cook you some rice. But remember, NO biscuits for elevenses. They're bad for your teeth."

They groaned even more loudly. But Mum took no notice, just grabbed her coat, and left.

Dad shrugged. "Better do as we're told, kids."

Kitty stuck out her teeth, held two fingers above her head like ears and hopped around. "I'll turn into a bunny if I eat any more lettuce, Dad!" she said.

He laughed, and sent them out into the garden to play while he did the washing up.

The morning passed quickly. Daniel and Kitty played hide-and-seek with William and Sally, the children next door, until heavy clouds made the sky dark. Kitty shivered.

"It's going to rain," said Sally. "Come in for a snack."

Her mother gave them a plate of chocolate biscuits to share, and glasses of lemonade. Daniel winked at Kitty.

As lunchtime came near they decided they should go home. It had stopped raining, but the air was damp and cold. "Lovely weather for salad," Kitty groaned.

They were surprised to see a strange man sitting at the kitchen table with Dad. They each had a glass of beer. Dad looked very pleased. He told the children this was a very old friend he hadn't seen for years. The man, whose name was Bill, was big and jolly. He looked at his watch, "Well, if your lady-wife isn't coming home, why don't we all go down the road and get fish and chips?"

The children jumped up and down, screaming with delight, and clapping their hands.

Dad looked at them, then at the fridge door, then at his watch. "We-ell . . ."

"Oh, come on!" said Bill.

"You'd better promise not to tell your Mum," said Dad.

"We won't!" yelled Kitty.

Twenty minutes later they were all walking down the road, munching delicious fish and chips with their fingers. When they got back to

93

the house Bill took cans of fizzy drink from his pockets, which made a perfect end to the meal. The children were sorry when he had to go.

"Oh, dear," said Dad, looking at the mess of greasy newspaper and empty cans on the kitchen table. "We'd better clean up. Mum will be back in half an hour."

When Mum's key turned in the lock, Dad and Daniel were watching a film on television, and Kitty was wheeling Mr. Tubs up and down the hall on her old baby tricycle.

Mum kissed her. "Hello, love, have you had a lovely day?"

Kitty nodded. She started to feel a bit guilty.

"And it wasn't *so* bad to have salad for lunch, was it?" asked Mum.

Kitty looked at her and went red. It was no good. She couldn't tell fibs—that would be terrible. So she told Mum what had happened.

"Aha—he did, did he?" said Mum, folding her arms, a little smile curling at the corner of her mouth. She marched into the sitting room.

"Well, was it good, having a salad of fish and chips?" she asked, standing in between Dad and the TV.

Dad looked really guilty. He glanced sideways at Kitty, and she could almost hear him thinking, "*But you promised you wouldn't tell.*"

"Don't be cross with Dad," she said.

At that, a big grin broke across Mum's face. "Look at you all!" she said. "Like frightened rabbits! You obviously *have* been eating too many greens. Well, if you must know I went to the market to get a special treat for tonight's supper, and I met Bill—which was a lovely surprise. And he told me about your lunch."

"And you don't mind?"asked Dad.

"Course not. I'm not a witch, you know! Didn't I say I'm making something you like for supper?"

"What is it, Mum?" asked Kitty.

"Fish and chips!" said Mum.

"Oh, no!" they all groaned. And then they started to laugh.

THE CASE OF
THE SMELL

Traditional Chinese
retold by Mark Cohen

In the far northwest of China there lived Effendi Nasreddin. He was the cleverest man for miles around, and many people came to ask his advice. Once a very poor man came to see him for just this reason. He bowed very low and very humbly, and said: "I hardly dare to beg you to help someone who is as poor and unworthy as I am. But I have a great favor to ask of you."

"I shall be delighted if I can be of help to you. So tell me what I can do," replied the Effendi.

The poor man sighed. "Life is hard for people as poor as I am. Yesterday I was passing the door of that restaurant owned by Lord Enibi. I paused for a moment because the food smelled

96

so delicious. Lord Enibi himself pounced on me. He said he had caught me swallowing the smell of his food, and handed me a bill! As you can imagine, I hadn't a single penny to pay him. So he dragged me before the judge. Judge Cadi said he needed to sleep on the case, but he is going to pass sentence today. Could you possibly come along to the court and say something in my defense?"

"Of course, I'll come to the court with you," said the Effendi, "and see what I can do to help."

When they reached the court, Lord Enibi and Judge Cadi were already there, talking and laughing together. But as soon as the judge saw the poor man, he suddenly looked solemn. "You should be ashamed of yourself," he shouted angrily. "You have filled yourself up with the smells from Lord Enibi's restaurant. But you haven't paid him a penny. Pay him what you owe him at once, do you hear!"

The Effendi stepped forward and bowed the deepest of bows. "It so happens that this poor man is my younger brother. He hasn't a cent, so I've come along to settle his debt."

Then he took a bulging purse that hung on his belt. He held it up to Lord Enibi's ear and shook it till all the coins jingled inside.

"Can you hear the money rattling then, my lord?" said the Effendi cheerfully.

"Don't be silly! I'm not deaf. Of course I can hear it," replied Lord Enibi crossly.

"Excellent. I'm so glad that is settled. The debt is canceled, of course. My brother smelled your food cooking and now you have heard his money jingling. So that puts things straight between you."

And with that, Effendi Nasreddin turned on his heel and gave the poor man his arm. Together they walked out of the court.

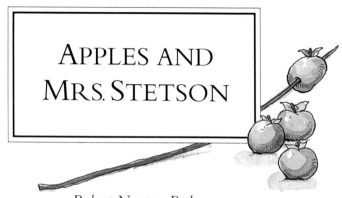

APPLES AND
MRS. STETSON

Robert Newton Peck

Soup was my best pal. His real and righteous name was Luther Wesley Vinson, but nobody called him Luther. He didn't like it. I called him Luther just once, which prompted Soup to break me of a very bad habit before it really got formed. As soon as the swelling went out of my lip, I called him Soup instead of Thoop.

He first discouraged his mother of the practice of calling him Luther. (Using a different method, of course.) She used to call him home to mealtime by yelling, "Luther!" But he never answered to the name. He'd rather miss supper. When his mother got wise, she'd stand out on their back porch, cup her hands to her mouth, and yell, "Soup's on!"

From a distance (their farm was uproad next to ours) all you could hear was "Soup." And that was how the kids who were playing ball in the pasture started thinking his name was Soup, because he answered to it.

When it came to getting the two of us in trouble, Soup was a regular genius. He liked to whip apples. But that was nothing new. Every kid did. The apples had to be small and green and hard, about the size of a golf ball. The whip had to be about four to five foot long, with a point on the small end that you'd whittle sharp with your jackknife. You held the apple close to your chest with your left hand and pushed the pointed stick into the apple, but not so far as it'd come out the yonder side. No matter how careful you speared the apple, a few drops of juice would squirt on your shirt. They dried to small, tiny brown spots that never even came out in the wash.

Sassafras made the best whips. You could swing a sassafras whip through the air so fast it would whistle. The apple would fly off, and you'd think it would never come down. To whip an apple was sport enough for most of us, but not for old Soup.

"Watch this," he said.

"What?" I said.

We were up in the apple orchard on a hillside

that overlooked town. Below us was the Baptist church.

"I bet I can hit the Baptist church."

"You better not, Soup."

"Why not?"

"We'll really catch it."

"No we won't. And what's more, I bet this apple can hit the bell in the bell tower and make it ring."

"Aw, it won't go that far."

"Oh, no?"

Soup whipped his apple, and I was right. It landed far short of the Baptist church.

"Watch me," I said. And with my next throw I almost hit the church roof.

"My turn," said Soup.

I'll have to admit that Soup put all he had into his next throw. The whip made a whistle that would've called a dead dog. That old apple took off like it'd been shot out of a gun, made a big arc through the sky, and for a few long seconds I thought we'd hear that old bell ring for sure.

But we never heard the sounding brass. What we heard was the tinkling cymbal of a broken window. Breaking a pane of plain old glass wasn't stylish enough for Soup. It had to be stained glass. Even the sound of that stained glass shattering had color in it. I just stood there

looking at that tiny little black star of emptiness that was once a window pane. It was like somebody busted my heart.

"No," I said, in almost a whisper.

I wanted the glass to fly up into place again, like it never happened. So that the little black star would erase away like a bad dream. But there it was and there it stayed.

"No," said Soup.

My feet were stuck to the ground like I was standing in twin buckets of mortar. I couldn't run. Not even when a lady ran out of the side door of the church and pointed up at us. Even though she was far below, it felt like her finger took a stab into my chest. It was a pain, just like when you get stuck with the tip of a sword.

To make matters worse, it was Mrs. Stetson.

My family wasn't Baptist. But I guess that she knew Mama and Aunt Carrie real well, because she came to call almost every week. Religion was her favorite subject. You'd be hard put to find a soul who knew more about God than Mrs. Stetson. She was a walking, talking Bible, which she could quote chapter and verse. Get her started and it went on like rain. Forty days and forty nights. Just to be in the same room with Mrs. Stetson was like being caught in a downpour. She sure could drench a body with scripture.

But what she was saying now was far from holy. And if there was anything Mrs. Stetson was poor at, it was talking as she climbed full-speed up a steep hill. By the time she reached me, she was so out of breath from the uphill scolding that she couldn't say a word.

I looked around for Soup, but he was gone. Good old Soup. So there I stood, with a sassafras stick in my hand and apple-juice spots on the front of my shirt. Still wet. The mortar in my shoes had now hardened into stone. My ears were ringing with a *tinkle tinkle tinkle* of smashing glass that wouldn't seem to stop.

"You!" she said.

"Me?"

Her eyes burned with the wrath of the Old Testament. It was plain to behold that Mrs. Stetson believed that you had to smite trans-gressors so that the ground ran red with their blood until the multitudes were sore afraid. Especially sore. But if anybody ever looked sore, it was Mrs. Stetson.

"Robert Peck!" she said in full voice.

Her big old hands shot out and grabbed my face and my hair. She shook me hard enough to shake off one of my shoes. Then after she stopped shaking me, she twisted my head around so my nose was pointing right at the little black star of that broken window pane.

"Just look what you did!" said Mrs. Stetson. "Look me in the eye and tell the truth. Do you dare say you didn't?"

"I didn't."

This was not the response that she expected. I guess what she really sought was an outburst of guilt, a tear-soaked plea to ask for the forgiveness of God and Mrs. Stetson—perhaps not in that order of importance.

"I didn't. Honest, Mrs. Stetson. I didn't throw an apple that far. Look how far it is."

"You *did* do it. I saw you do it. And here's the apple you did it with." She had a pierced apple in one hand and my switch in the other, and I knew I was a goner.

"But I couldn't hit the church from way up here. Nobody could."

"Bosh! Even a fool knows how far an apple will pitch from a stick. Watch."

You won't believe what I saw. Mrs. Stetson somehow let go of her senses. She pushed an apple on a stick, and before I could grab her arm, her temper bested reason. Whissshh! You never saw a worse throw in your life, not if you stood up in that old orchard from now until Judgment. Her apple never even headed in the direction of the Baptist church. Nowhere near. But you couldn't say that apple didn't have any steam to it. No, sir. It flew off her stick (my stick) like a rifle ball, going east by northeast, and finally tipped over a flowerpot with a geranium in it outside old Haskin's shack window. And the pot cracked the glass.

Crash-tinkle!

Out came old Mr. Haskin with blood in his eye. His language would have made Satan himself cover his ears. Not really fancy swearing, just a long string of old favorites. He pointed at Mrs. Stetson and me, then he started uphill and coming our way fast.

"Run!" yelled Mrs. Stetson. "That man's a degenerate."

We ran, Mrs. Stetson and I. She had on two shoes and I wore one, which evened the speed a bit, and we ran as if Hell was a step behind. We ran until we could no longer hear the terrible things that old Haskin shouted he would do to Mrs. Stetson the next time she came near

his rotten old shack. We didn't stop running, Mrs. Stetson and I, until we darted into Frank Rooker's garage and had bolted the door.

But as we ran in, Soup ran out, after taking one look at Mrs. Stetson. Out the side door he shot, into the arms of Mr. Haskin. Soup still had his switch in hand, and his shirt-front was smelled and spotted with apple juice, which was enough evidence for old Haskin. Borrowing the sassafras switch, the old man gave Soup a fine smarting. I'll have to admit it sure must have been a sight to see.

From where Mrs. Stetson and I stood panting, we didn't see it. But we heard it all. Thinking I'd be next, I even winced for poor Soup with every blow. Best of all, we heard him confess up to breaking the window, even though it wasn't the same glass he got thrashed for. In a way, it really was justice.

Mrs. Stetson was right. There really is a God.

POSY BATES
– INVENTOR

Helen Cresswell

Posy Bates was sitting up in her room thinking. She did quite a lot of this, for an eight-year-old. Not that anyone else believed it—especially grown-ups.

"I just wish you'd stop and think, Posy," Daff was always saying.

"Do you ever *think* what you're doing?" Miss Perlethorpe would sigh.

This particular day Posy Bates was thinking about thinking. This had been triggered off by watching a man on television showing how to make things out of empty yogurt cartons. He had made desk-tidies, spill-holders, keyrings, mobiles—he had gone on and on. By the time he was finished, Posy thought it very likely that the whole world could be made out of empty yogurt pots.

This had set her thinking. In the past she herself had made all kinds of things from cornflake packets, yogurt pots, matchboxes and jam jars. On Daff's dressing table there still stood a decorated jar for cotton wool balls that Posy had made once for Mothering Sunday. But so far, everything she had made had come from an idea of Miss Perlethorpe's or a television program.

Now, Posy was so enchanted by the infinite possibilities of yogurt pots that she had decided to change the world.

"You don't *have* to put coal in a coal bucket," she thought. "You could plant a tree in it, or take it shopping, instead of a basket. And you don't *have* to use blankets on your bed. You could cut them up into small squares and use them as kettle holders."

There seemed no limit to what you could do if you really thought about it. And Posy Bates meant to think about it. She intended, in short, to become an inventor.

"I reckon being an inventor's the next best thing to being a witch," she told Peg the Leg. "Absolutely total."

He, being a stick insect, did not respond. He was the fifth Peg the Leg she had had so far this year. Posy yearned for a pet, but Daff put her foot down, and said no. So Posy was reduced to a procession of spiders, snails, ladybugs, stick insects, hedgehogs—anything that moved, really. (The only things she had drawn the line at so far were worms. Even Posy Bates could not see *them* as pets.)

But she knew very well that it is not kind to keep such things in jam jars and boxes. So she kept them only a few days, then set them free. Then she found some more, and kept them instead. And as one spider looks very like another (except perhaps to its own mother) and one stick insect like the next, she always gave them the same names. Then she could pretend they *were* the same—real pets.

"Better get started straightaway, then," she remarked to Punch and Judy. They showed as much interest as you would expect a pair of spiders to show.

"Now, what first?"

"Posy!"

It was Daff calling, and already half-way up the stairs by the sound of it.

"Oh, bumboils!"

Posy scrambled out of the cupboard and shut the door. She managed to

be sitting innocently on her bed, reading, when Daff poked her head around the door.

"Oh, there you are! Nose in a book, as usual."

Privately, Posy thought that in a book was the best place for any nose to be, but wisely said nothing.

"I want you to fetch me some things from the shop. Come along, now, look sharp!"

She was gone. Posy followed her, wondering how to look sharp. She didn't see how anyone could actually *look* sharp, even if they were.

"Here's the list."

Posy took it, and the money, and went out.

"A bag!" Daff called after her. "You'll want a bag!"

"Oh no I won't!" thought Posy. She fished the metal coal bucket out of the shed. Then she scooted off, before Daff could call again.

She enjoyed the novel feeling of swinging a coal bucket instead of a bag or basket. It creaked and rattled and was more company, somehow. It also made the boring business of being sent up to the shop seem actually rather exciting, fun even.

"It's not a bucket or a bag or a basket, it's a baskle, busket, bagget, bugget . . ."

"Hey wait, Posy!"

It was Sam Post running after her.

"Where are you going?"

"Shop."

"What've you got *that* for, then?" he asked, pointing at the bucket.

"Put things in," Posy told him airily.

"*Put* things in? What, the shopping, you mean?"

"Course."

"But what *for*? You don't get coal, not at the shop."

"I'm not getting coal. I'm getting gravy powder, a dozen eggs, half a pound of bacon and a pound of sausages."

"And you're putting them in *there*?"

"I told you." Posy stopped. "Look—what's the difference between a coal bucket and a basket?"

He stared.

"There isn't one. They've both got handles and they both hold things. There!" Posy was triumphant.

"But . . . you use baskets for shopping and coal buckets for coal."

"You might," Posy told him loftily. "I don't."

She was tempted to add "Because I'm an inventor," but decided not to. If Sam couldn't catch on to the coal bucket idea, he wasn't going to catch on to the other things she had in mind. Or that she *vaguely* had in mind. She rather wished Sam would go away and leave her in peace, to think up her inventions.

"Well, I'm not going into the shop with you carrying that!" said Sam.

"Nobody asked you," said Posy sweetly, and watched him run off.

It was just her luck that Miss Perlethorpe should be in the Post Office, buying stamps. Posy and her bucket came creaking and clanking in and Miss Perlethorpe turned around.

"Oh Posy, it's you. Thank you, Mrs. Parkins."

Miss Perlethorpe began sorting through her letters and sticking her stamps.

"Now Posy, what is it you wanted?"

Silently Posy handed over her list. One by one Mrs. Parkins fetched and weighed out the items. Posy prayed that Miss Perlethorpe would go before she had to pay and put the things in her bucket. Something told her that Miss Perlethorpe would not see the point of going shopping with a coal bucket.

But Miss Perlethorpe did not go. She stuck on the stamps with a maddening slowness, and then began looking at the various leaflets on the Post Office counter.

"There we are, then!" said Mrs. Parkins. "Got your basket, dear?"

She went to the till, and Posy snatched up the things from the counter and dropped them

114

into the bucket.

"Thank you!" She grabbed the change and made for the door, bucket clanking.

"Posy!"

She froze.

"Whatever . . .? A *bucket*?"

"Here we go again!" thought Posy wearily.

She turned and faced Miss Perlethorpe.

The conversation she then had was almost exactly the same as the one she had just had with Sam. Except that now there was Mrs. Parkins too, with her "Well I nevers!" and "Would you believes!"

At the end, Miss Perlethorpe said, "If you are going to be an inventor, Posy, there are several things I would like to suggest. I wish you would invent a way of keeping your exercise books tidy, and getting to school on time. I also wish you would invent something to keep your hair tidy and your shoes clean. And it is to be hoped that coal dust does not get into your mother's bacon."

Posy stamped home, clanking and glowering.

She went to see if Fred was awake. The good thing about him was that genius or not, he never answered back or criticized. Even when he bawled it was nothing personal.

He lay cocooned in his pram under the wide green shelter of the orchard.

"Going to be an inventor, Fred," she told him.

He gazed up with calm blue eyes. "You know— invent new things."

He did not seem excited. The trouble was, Posy thought, that being a baby, most things were new to him anyway.

"There are millions of things he hasn't seen yet," she thought. "Not even on the telly."

This was an amazing thought.

"Don't worry, Fred," she told him. "I'll make sure you're clued up. I bet you're already the most clued-up baby in Little Paxton—in England, for all I know, England, Europe, the world, the universe!"

At this point Fred, disappointingly, shut his eyes.

"Oh well," said Posy.

She did not wish to have the bucket conversation with Daff, so put the shopping into a plastic bag and left it on the draining board, then went up to her hidey hole to think.

Being an inventor was not as easy as Posy had thought. She could think of things, she'd like to invent, all right, but didn't know how to make them. She sat on her nest in the cupboard and made a list of the ten things she would most like to invent:

1. A brainwashing machine to make Mom let me have a dog.

2. A brainwashing machine to stop Mom picking on me.

3. A brainwashing machine to make Pearly forget to go to school each day.

4. A special whistle to make birds come and feed out of your hand.

5. A calendar with no Sundays.

6. An everlasting ice cream.

7. An everlasting gobstopper.

8. A calendar with Christmas every month.

9. A special dye to make my hair exactly the same color as Emma Hawksworth.

10. A dream machine.

She stared at the list long and hard and chewed on her pencil. It seemed very clear that none of these items could be made out of yogurt pots.

"Don't know how to make *any* of them," she admitted to Punch and Judy. "Perhaps what I need to be is a witch, not an inventor."

She sighed deeply. She did not, however, give up. She decided to try a different approach.

"What I'll do is not invent new things," she thought. "I'll leave that till I'm grown up. What I'll do is invent new ways to use things that have already been invented. Like using the coal bucket as a shopping basket. Now . . . what shall I start with?"

She looked thoughtfully at Punch and Judy and Peg the Leg, but could not think of a single use for them.

"Except to put in Pearly's desk and frighten the life out of her," she thought. "Trouble is, it'd frighten the life out of *them*, as well. Cruelty to spiders and stick insects, that'd be."

So she climbed out of the cupboard and looked around her room. What should she choose? Everything looked exceedingly boring and everyday, and to be used for one purpose and one purpose only. Still Posy did not give up.

"What I'll do, I'll shut my eyes and spin

around. Then I'll open them, and the first thing I see, I'll invent a new way to use it. Even if it takes me all day to think of something."

So she closed her eyes and spun and opened her eyes again and the first thing she saw was a sock.

"Oh, *gubbins*!" said Posy Bates.

She sat on the bed and looked coldly at the sock, which was pink-and-white striped and looked like exactly what it was a sock.

"That," she said, "is just my luck."

But she had set herself a test.

"You couldn't wear it on your head as a hat," she thought, "not unless your head shrunk."

The minutes ticked by on her Mickey Mouse clock.

"You couldn't use it as a pencil case. It hasn't got a zipper."

Tick tock tick tock. "You couldn't blow it up, like a balloon."

Posy was making a very respectable list of things for which the

119

sock couldn't be used. She supposed that made her the opposite of an inventor, whatever that was.

"A sock," she thought glumly, "is a sock. Full stop."

Under her window she heard Fred begin to bawl.

"He's all bawl and bottle!" Posy said disgustedly, and was so pleased with the sound of it that she said it again, "Bawl and bottle!"

And then she had the inspiration.

"Yipee!"

She snatched up the sock and ran out of her room and down the stairs. Daff was changing Fred's nappy. On the table stood his bottle, ready for the feed.

Posy picked it up and pulled on the sock. Perfect—it fitted like a glove—or a sock. It was, quite clearly, a bottle-sockle.

"There!"

Daff turned.

"Whatever?"

"Bottle-sockle!" Posy told her, triumphant. "New invention! You know, like a tea cozy or an egg cozy. You're always saying the milk gets cold before he's finished."

"But where's it *been*?" cried Daff. "You were *wearing* that yesterday!"

Reluctantly Posy peeled the sock off the

bottle. It did look rather grimy, now she looked at it.

"All right," she said. "But it is a good idea. It'd be perfect."

"As a matter of fact," said Daff slowly, "it is a good idea. A very good idea. You run up and fetch a clean sock, Posy, and we'll use that."

Posy raced back up to her room and rummaged for a clean sock.

"I did it!" she told her pets. "I invented!"

And after that Fred's bottle always had a bottle-sockle. And after that it didn't matter when odd socks went missing. Instead of grumbling, as she always had, Daff would toss the odd one into Fred's basket, saying,

"Here we are—another bottle cozy!"

"Sockle!" Posy would tell her. "Bottle-sockle!"

But it did not really matter. Sockle or cozy—what was the difference? Posy Bates was an inventor.

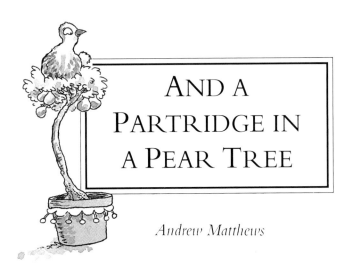

AND A
PARTRIDGE IN
A PEAR TREE

Andrew Matthews

It was Christmas Eve and Prince Truelove was terribly nervous. He paced the Royal Chamber restlessly, or gazed anxiously at the logs blazing in the Royal Hearth. Outside in the courtyard, a choir sang carols, but the Prince hardly heard a note. All he could hear was Princess Debbie's voice and when he looked into the fire the glowing embers seemed to form the shape of her face. In fact, the Prince was so deep in daydreams about the Princess that he did not notice the Royal Chamberlain enter the room.

"A-hem!" the Chamberlain coughed discreetly. "I have brought a map of the procession for your perusal, Your Highness!"

Eagerly, the Prince examined the unrolled parchment. A concerned look crossed his face.

"Look here!" he cried, pointing. "There's a place called 'Troll Bridge.' There's a picture of a troll next to it—and next to the troll there's some writing that says 'Beware of the Troll.' What does all this mean, Chamberlain?"

"It means that a troll lives under the bridge, Your Highness," the Chamberlain replied.

"B-but trolls . . . eat people, don't they?" shuddered the Prince.

"That is their custom, I believe, Your Highness," said the Chamberlain calmly, "but to take any other road would add a day to the journey. Besides, it is a well-known fact that trolls sleep through the winter months."

The Prince looked relieved at this news, then started pacing up and down again.

"I'm sure that my Christmas present will please Princess Debbie so much, she'll marry me at once!" he said. "Is everything exactly as I explained?"

"Not . . . exactly, Your Highness," said the Chamberlain gravely. "The swans, geese, calling birds, and French hens are just as you required. The Royal Gamekeeper has succeeded in training a partridge to stay in a pear tree. The Royal

Goldsmith has made five exceptionally beautiful rings, inscribed as you requested. The milkmaids, drummers, and dancing ladies are ready and waiting . . . only . . ."

"What?" demanded the Prince.

"The leaping lords, Your Highness. Only eleven remain," admitted the Chamberlain. "There were twelve originally, but Lord McSnurt has come down with gout and there isn't a leap left in him."

The Prince began to tear at his hair.

"Only eleven?" he groaned. "That ruins everything! How can I send her eleven leaping lords on the twelfth day of Christmas? It'll look so stupid!"

"I'm sure that eleven will prove to be sufficient acrobatic aristocracy, Your Highness," murmured the Chamberlain.

From a far corner of the room came the chiming of the Royal Clock.

"Well, it's too late now!" snapped the Prince. "Eleven will have to do. But if it does not work, I shall blame you, Chamberlain. If Princess Debbie turns me down, I shall have your beard plucked out with tweezers!"

"Ah!" sighed the Chamberlain. "What it is to be young, and in love!"

The procession set off at one-thirty exactly. The Prince had intended the journey to be a dignified affair, but it did not turn out quite as he had imagined. The French hens and calling birds squawked and whistled, the swans and geese hissed, the milkmaids giggled and the cows mooed loudly. Then came the drummers, the pipers, the dancing ladies, and the leaping lords who, as they leaped, shouted, "Whee!" and "Boing!" and "Yippee!" All the sounds together made an awful racket.

At the front of the procession, the Prince leaned across his horse and tugged the Chamberlain's sleeve.

"It's a bit noisy, isn't it?" he yelled. "Perhaps I should have stuck to quiet presents, like the five gold rings!"

"I'm sure Princess Debbie will be quite charmed, Your Highness," smiled the Chamberlain.

The procession was so loud that people could hear it a mile off and they gathered at the roadside to stare in openmouthed wonder. Prince Truelove felt embarrassed, but the thought of Princess Debbie's flashing eyes gave him the courage to go on.

The road threaded its way through a wood, then steepened as it climbed up to a narrow mountain pass. The noise of the procession echoed and reechoed off the sides of the mountains until the Prince's head began to ache and spin.

"I can't stand it!" he groaned.

"Take heart, Your Highness!" urged the Chamberlain. "See, a short way ahead lies Troll Bridge! It's all downhill after that!"

Troll Bridge spanned a deep chasm. Far below it, a mountain torrent raged its way around huge, jagged boulders. Prince True-love, who was not fond of heights, shut his eyes and gripped his reins tightly.

No sooner had his horse taken one step on

to the bridge than there came the sound of a
bellow so loud that the entire procession fell
silent.

"Oi!" bawled a voice. "What's all the noise
about?"

The Prince opened his eyes wide. To his
horror, an enormous and fearsomely ugly troll
clambered up on to the far end of the bridge,
blocking the way.

"What's this lot, then?" roared the troll.
"Ain't you got no consideration? You've
disturbed me 'ibernation!" The troll drew a
spiked club from his belt and tested the sharp-
ness of the spikes against his thumb.

"Troll!" called the Prince. "This procession
my Christmas present to Princess Debbie and—"

"Why didn't you buy 'er a new dress or a box o' chocolates like anyone else would?" scoffed the troll.

"And," continued the Prince, ignoring the troll's interruption, "if you don't stand aside immediately, I shall . . . I shall . . ."

"Yeah?" said the troll.

"You will incur the Royal Displeasure," said the Chamberlain, "and a proclamation about you will be read aloud in every village!"

"'Ow terrible!" laughed the troll. "Why, I'm tremblin' in me boots at the very idea!" He pointed his club straight at the Prince. "You look like you'd make a tasty suet puddin', me lad!" he growled. "And as for you," he squinted at the Chamberlain, "you look a bit on the tough side. I think I'll pickle you for later! Now I'm awake, I could just do with a toothsome trollish snack!"

The troll began to cross the bridge.

"Chamberlain!" squeaked the Prince. "Think of something!"

"I am sorely tempted to suggest that we flee faster than the wind, Your Highness," said the Chamberlain, "but I fear that trolls are well known for their athletic prowess."

And that gave the Prince a splendid idea. He looked the troll squarely in the face and said loudly, "Can you run?"

The troll found the question so astonishing that he stood still in the middle of the bridge.

"Run?" he frowned. "Course I can run! Gotta keep fit in my game, y' know! You'd be amazed 'ow fast people goes when they got an 'ungry troll be'ind 'em!"

"And how about swimming?" asked the Prince hurriedly.

"Like a fish!" said the troll proudly.

"But can you leap?" Prince Truelove inquired.

"Watch this!" said the troll. He tucked his club back under his belt, crouched for a second,

and then performed the most tremendous backward somersault, landing on the far side of the chasm.

The milkmaids, ladies, and lords burst into applause and the troll bowed.

"Piece o' cake!" he mumbled. "No, really, it was nothin'!"

Just before the applause died down, the Prince raised his hand for silence.

"I've got an offer you can't refuse," he told the troll. "I'm a leaping lord short and you seem to have a talent for leaping. If you'll join the procession, I'll make you a lord!"

"Well, well!" gasped the troll, scratching his head. "Me, a lord! Cor, that'd be somethin' to tell the other trolls, wouldn't it?" A cunning gleam came into his eyes. "What about me ravenous 'unger, then?"

"Fear not!" exclaimed the Chamberlain. "For, where we are bound, a sumptuous feast of delicate dainties awaits!"

"Eh?" puzzled the troll.

"We're goin' to a knees-up!" shouted one of the pipers. "There'll be plenty o' posh nosh!"

"Sounds dead wicked!" rumbled the troll, smacking his lips. "OK, it's a deal!"

"Kneel down and I shall dub you!" Prince Truelove commanded. He rode across the bridge to where the troll waited, sunk down on to one knee. Even so, he was as tall as the Prince's horse. Prince Truelove drew his sword and touched the flat of the blade on the troll's shoulder. "Arise . . . er, what's your name?"

"Doug," said the troll.

"Arise, Lord Doug!" proclaimed the Prince.

And in the end, it was Lord Doug who did the trick. For, as Princess Debbie explained to

her lady-in-waiting later, any Prince who went to the trouble of taming a troll as a Christmas present must be suffering from a bad attack of true love.

In fact, the Prince's attack of true love was so bad that it spread. The eleven leaping lords proposed to the dancing ladies and were accepted. All the drummers and the pipers who were not already married found themselves betrothed to the milkmaids. Everybody decided that they would wed on the same day as Prince Truelove and Princess Debbie.

As for Lord Doug, he went back to the mountains to finish his hibernation. But the following spring, he awoke a changed troll. He gave up eating people completely and turned vegetarian.

"Well, it's like this," he said, when any of his fellow trolls asked him about it. "I'm a lord now. I got me dignity to think of, ain't I? When you're a member of the upper class, you can't be caught eatin' riff-raff, mate!"

HARRY'S
AUNT

Sheila Lavelle

When Harry went to stay with his Aunt Winnie for the holidays he didn't know she was a witch.

She didn't look like a witch at all.

It wasn't until after supper that Harry found out.

Aunt Winnie put on a black cloak and a pointed hat. She took an old broomstick from the cupboard and went for a ride around the garden in the moonlight.

Harry couldn't believe his eyes.

The next day Aunt Winnie turned into a chimpanzee in the greengrocer's store. She climbed on to a shelf and threw oranges and bananas at the surprised customers.

The greengrocer went mad with rage.

On the way home Aunt Winnie turned into

an elephant, on the Number Five bus. It took six men to get her free.

"Double fare for an elephant," said the driver. And he made Harry pay an extra fifty pence.

In the Post Office on Friday Aunt Winnie turned into a crocodile. Everybody ran into the street, screaming and shouting.

"I'm fed up with this," said Harry.

"I can't help it, Harry," said his aunt. "I've been changing into all sorts of things for so long I can't stop. We had better stay at home for a few days."

Harry agreed. He took the dead bats and toads out of the larder and threw them in the dustbin.

On Saturday, Aunt Winnie planted poison ivy in the flowerbed. Harry mowed the lawn, keeping a watchful eye on his aunt. She might turn herself into a beetle and fall down a crack in the ground.

Then Mr. Mills came by with his dog, Horace.

"Not going to the Dog Show?" he said, looking over the fence. "Village Hall. Two o'clock." And he trotted away.

Aunt Winnie looked at Harry.

Harry looked at Aunt Winnie.

"No," said Harry. "We are *not* going to the Dog Show. It's better if we stay at home."

"But I can't stay at home all my life!" wailed Aunt Winnie. "I'll turn into a cabbage!"

"*That* will make a nice change," said Harry to himself.

But Aunt Winnie got her own way. She put on her yellow hat with the poppies on it.

Harry kept close to her all the way to the Village Hall.

He had a funny feeling in his tummy. It was a bit like going to the dentist . . . only worse.

The Village Hall was packed. Harry had never seen so many dogs in his life. He had never heard such a din.

At one end of the Hall was the judge's table, covered in silver cups.

"Well I never," said Aunt Winnie. "There's dear old Mrs. Moon."

And she disappeared into the crowd.

"Come back!" shouted Harry.

But his aunt was nowhere to be seen.

Harry climbed onto a chair to look over the heads of the crowd.

Suddenly there was trouble. Dogs ran round the Hall barking and howling. Chairs were knocked over. Benches crashed to the floor. Someone screamed.

Harry stood on tiptoe to see what the trouble was.

It was a cat—a small black cat, ears back and tail bushed out. It dashed from table to table, along the windowsills, over a row of cages, spitting and hissing at the dogs behind it.

"Oh no! Aunt Winnie's done it again," said Harry.

People were rushing about, trying to catch their dogs.

The judge's table fell over with a crash, and the silver cups rolled all over the floor.

The cat started to climb up the curtains behind the stage.

Harry saw his chance.

He leaped down from the chair and pushed through the crowd.

Harry reached up and grabbed the cat by the scruff of the neck, and pushed his way out the side door.

Harry's sleeve was torn, his trousers were ripped and his face was scratched and dirty.

"That's it, Aunt Winnie," he told the cat. "I'm never going anywhere with you ever again."

And he ran all the way back to his aunt's cottage, with the cat tucked into his jacket.

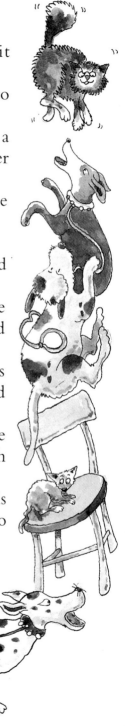

Harry dumped the cat on the rug in front of the fire. He sat in the rocking chair to wait for his aunt to turn back into herself again.

Nothing happened.

The cat dozed off in the warmth of the fire.

Harry prodded the cat with his toe.

"Come on, Aunt Winnie," he said crossly. "You can't stay like that for ever. It's nearly tea-time."

Just when he was getting really worried, Harry heard a bang at the door. He opened it, and his eyes grew round as dinner plates.

On the doorstep stood a large black and white dog. In its teeth was a silver cup.

Harry stared.

Then a most extraordinary thing happened.

The dog's back legs and tail disappeared. In their place were Aunt Winnie's galoshes and her old green skirt.

Then the dog's front legs and furry body disappeared. There was Aunt Winnie's orange cardigan.

Last of all the big black and white head dis-

appeared. And there was Aunt Winnie's smiling face, and the yellow hat with the poppies on it.

"Aunt Winnie!" cried Harry. "I thought you'd turned into a cat."

"I wouldn't do a silly thing like that," said Aunt Winnie. "I turned into a dog and won First Prize!"

She put the silver cup proudly on the shelf above the fireplace.

Harry looked at the cat, still sleeping by the fire.

"What are we going to do with that?" he said.

"Keep it, of course," said Aunt Winnie.

"I've always wanted a black cat."

And she took her broomstick from the cupboard and went for a ride over the rooftops before tea.

DIRTY
DILLY

Tony Bradman

There are four of us in my family. First of all, there's my mother and my father. And there's me, of course. I'm their oldest child, their daughter. My name is Dorla. That makes three, doesn't it?

And then, last but certainly not least, there's Dilly, my little brother.

I suppose I shouldn't say so, but when Dilly was a baby I didn't like him very much. Once, not long after he was born, I even asked Mother to take him back to the hospital where she got him. Well, he did cry a lot, after all.

I love Dilly now though, I really do. He doesn't cry like a baby anymore, although he can make plenty of noise when he feels like it. He can be a lot of fun, too, but sometimes he can be a real problem, as you'll see.

Part of the trouble is that Dilly can be very,

140

very stubborn. When he decides to do something, it's hard to get him to change his mind.

For instance, Dilly used to like water more than anything else in the whole world. He loved to play pouring-out games, and splashing games, and getting-as-wet-as-you-can games all the time. In fact, Father said that Dilly liked water a little *too* much.

"Every time he has a bath," said Father, "I finish up wetter than him!"

But Mother and I were sure that Father enjoyed those getting-wet games as much as Dilly—even though he wouldn't admit it.

Then just the other morning, when he got up, Dilly decided that he didn't like water after all. He told Mother that he didn't want to brush his teeth, or wash, or have a bath, or play with water.

Mother was confused.

"That's strange, Dilly," she said. "I thought water was your favorite thing. Why don't you like it anymore?"

Dilly looked very stubborn.

"I just don't, that's all," he said.

"But Dilly," said Mother, "you'll get very dirty if you don't wash. Very dirty, and very smelly."

"I don't care," said Dilly, with his nose in the air. "I like dirt. I like dirt a lot." Dilly smiled. "In fact, dirt is now my favorite thing. And I don't care if I smell."

Mother looked hard at Dilly.

"Okay," she said at last. "Have it your way."

All that day, it seemed as if Dilly went out of his way to play the dirtiest games he could think of. He rolled in the dirt a lot, and by the evening he looked very grubby indeed.

Mother thought that Dilly would have forgotten all about not liking water by the time it came to having a bath before bed. So she was smiling when she called him in. She wasn't smiling for long, though.

"Come on, Dilly," she said. "Your bath is ready."

Dilly didn't stop rolling in the dirt.

"I'm not having a bath," he said. "I don't like water, remember?"

Now I could see from Mother's face that she was a little cross.

"Dilly Dinosaur," she said, "I think it's time we forgot all about this not washing business. You have got to have a bath. You can't possibly go to bed in that state."

"But I don't want a bath," said Dilly. "I don't

like water anymore."

"Dilly Dinosaur! Now you'll stop all this nonsense, come indoors, and get in that tub!"

Dilly didn't say anything for a moment. But I could tell from looking at his stubborn face what was coming next. He opened his mouth and let loose with his ultraspecial, 150-mile-per-hour superscream, the one that makes Mother wince, Father clap in his earplugs, and me hide under the bed.

When Dilly had finished, Mother and Father whispered to each other for a while. Afterward they told me that they had decided to let Dilly find out for himself what it really meant not to wash, or have a bath, or brush your teeth.

"Okay, Dilly," said Mother at the time. "Have it your way. Go to bed dirty."

And that's exactly what Dilly did.

Dilly didn't wash or brush his teeth the next morning, either. He just got dirtier, and dirtier, and dirtier. He played in the dirt all day, and in the evening, Father called him in.

"Now, Dilly," said Father. "Are you going to have a bath tonight or not?"

Dilly looked disgusting. There was food all round his mouth and down his front, and his teeth looked dreadful. But he still didn't want to have a bath. He looked at Father, and then opened his mouth the way he did when he was winding up to let loose an ultraspecial, 150-mile-per-hour superscream . . .

"Okay, okay, Dilly," said Father. "Have it your way. No bath again tonight. But you'll be sorry!"

Dilly just smiled.

The next day, Dilly's best friend Dixie was coming to play. She lives right next door, and Dilly just loves to play with her. Usually they play with water a lot, because Dixie loves water as much as Dilly does—or at least, as much as Dilly used to. She loves pouring-out games, and splashing games, and all those getting-as-wet-as-you-can games.

But that day, Dilly didn't want to play with water. He wanted Dixie to play his new favorite game—rolling in the dirt.

Dixie didn't want to. In fact, Dixie looked

Dixie didn't want to. In fact, Dixie looked really disappointed when Dilly said he didn't want to play any water games.

After a while, too, Dixie began to look at Dilly in a strange way. She looked, and she looked, and she looked. And she sniffed, too.

"Dilly," she said, "you look very funny. You're all dirty."

Dilly smiled proudly.

"That's because I don't like water anymore," he said. "I don't play with water, and I don't wash, or brush my teeth or have baths."

Dixie didn't smile.

"Dilly, you're smelly, too," she said. "You're a smelly Dilly, and I don't want to play with you today."

Dilly stopped smiling.

Not long after, Dixie said she wanted to go home. Dilly didn't say anything. But I could see that he had his thoughtful look on his face.

That evening, Mother called Dilly in. She didn't say anything about baths, or dirt, or washing. It was Dilly himself who brought up the subject.

"About water," he said, all of a sudden.

"Yes, Dilly?" said Mother.

"I think it's all right. I've decided I like it again."

He had, too. And he had that really stubborn look on his face, as well.

"Oh really?" was all that Mother said.

"In fact, water is my favorite thing," said Dilly. "Could I have a bath—*right now*?"

Mother looked at him very hard for a moment, trying hard not to smile.

"Okay, Dilly," she said at last. "Have it your way."

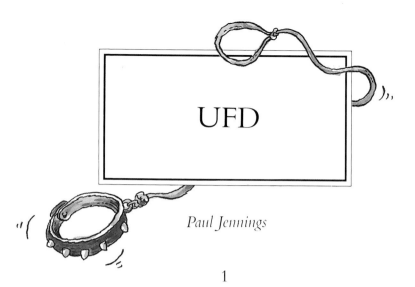

UFD

Paul Jennings

1

You can be the judge. Am I the biggest liar in the world or do I tell the truth? There is one thing for sure—Dad believes me. Anyway, I will leave it up to you. I will tell you what happened and you can make up your own mind.

It all starts one evening about teatime. Dad is cooking the dinner and Mum is watching *Sixty Minutes* on television. Suddenly there is a knock on the door. "I'll get it," yells my little brother Matthew. He always runs to be first to the door and first to the telephone. It really gets on my nerves the way he does this.

We hear the sound of Matthew talking to an adult. Then we hear heavy footsteps coming down the hall. Everyone looks up and stares at this man wearing a light blue uniform. He has

147

badges on his chest. One of them is a pair of little wings joined together. On his shoulder is a patch saying "ROYAL AUSTRALIAN AIR FORCE". We have never seen this man before.

"Yes?" says Dad.

"Mr. Hutchins?" says the man from the air force.

"Yes," answers Dad.

"Mr. Simon Hutchins?"

"No," says Dad pointing at me. "That is Simon Hutchins."

I can feel my face starting to go red. Everyone is looking at me. I think I know what this is about.

"I have come about the UFO," says the man in the uniform.

"UFO?" say Mum and Dad together.

"Yes," answers the guy in the uniform. "A

Mister Simon Hutchins rang the air force and reported a UFO."

Dad looks at me with a fierce expression on his face. He is about to blow his top. "This boy," says Dad slowly, "is the biggest liar in the world. You are wasting your time. He has not seen a UFO. He has dreamed it up. He is always making up the most fantastic stories. I am afraid you have come all this way for nothing."

"Nevertheless," says the man from the air force, "I will have to do a report. Do you mind if I talk to Simon?" Then he holds out his hand

to Dad. "My name is Wing Commander Collins."

"Go ahead," says Dad as he shakes Wing Commander Collins's hand. "And after you have finished I will have a talk to Simon myself. A very long talk." He gives me a dirty look. I know that I am in big trouble.

"What's a UFO?" butts in my little brother. Matthew doesn't know anything about anything. He is just a little kid with a big voice.

"It's an unidentified flying object," answers Wing Commander Collins.

"Wow," says Matthew with his mouth hanging open. "A flying saucer. Did you really see a flying saucer?"

"Not exactly," I say. "But I did see a UFO."

Wing Commander Collins sits down at the table and starts writing in a notebook. "What time did you see it?" he asks.

I think for a bit and then I say, "Seven o'clock this morning. I know it was seven o'clock because the boom gates on the railway line woke me up. The first train goes through at seven."

The Wing Commander writes this down. I don't know if he believes me or not. It is true though. Those boom gates go flying up after a train has gone through. They end up pointing at the sky. When they hit the buffer they make a terrific crash. They wake me up at seven every morning.

The air force man finishes writing and asks me his next question. "Where did you see it?"

I point through the kitchen window. "Out there. I was in bed and I saw it go past my window."

"How big was it?"

"About three feet."

He looks at me with a funny expression but he does not say anything. He just writes in his book. After a bit more writing he says, "And what color was it?"

"Black," I answer.

"And what was it made of?"

"Skin," I say. "Skin and hair."

At this point everyone in the room jumps to their feet and yells out, "Skin and hair?" as if they have never heard of skin and hair before.

"Yes," I say.

"And what shape was it?" growls the Commander.

"Dog-shaped. It was dog shaped."

"Dog-shaped?" yells the whole family again. I start to feel as if I am living with a bunch of parrots. They keep repeating everything I say.

"You mean," says the Wing Commander,

"that you saw a flying object that was shaped like a dog and covered in skin and hair?"

"No," I answer. "It wasn't a dog-shaped object. It was a dog-shaped dog. A real dog."

2

The Wing Commander springs to his feet and snaps his book shut. "Good grief," he shouts. "You mean I have come all this way on a Sunday night just because you looked out of the window and saw a dog?" The Wing Commander is getting mad.

"It was not just a dog," I tell him. "It was alive. And it was flying. It flew past the window and up over the house. It came from down there, down near the railway line."

Everyone looks down the hill but I can tell that no one believes me.

"Did it have wings?" says Matthew.

"No," I yell. "Of course not."

"Or a propeller?" says Dad in a mean voice.

"No," I shout. Tears are starting to come into my eyes.

"It was moving its legs. Like it was swimming in the air. Real fast. It was moving its legs and yapping."

The Wing Commander is leaving. He is charging down the hall. Before he goes he turns around and barks at Dad. "You had better teach that boy not to tell lies. Wasting people's time with this nonsense about a flying dog." He goes out and slams the front door behind him.

Mum and Dad and Matthew all stare at me. I can see that they don't believe a word of my story. I run to my bedroom and throw myself on the bed. I can hear Dad shouting from the kitchen. "You are grounded for two months Simon. I am sick of these stupid lies of yours. I am going to teach you a lesson about truthfulness once and for all."

I am sick of being called a liar.

I have tears in my eyes.

Dad comes into the bedroom and looks at me. He can see that I am not faking it. I am very upset. He starts to feel sorry for me. "Come on, Simon," he says. "You can't have seen a flying dog. It must have been a reflection in the window or something like that."

"I did," I shout at him. "I saw an unidentified flying dog—a UFD. I'll bet you a thousand dollars that I did."

"You haven't got a thousand dollars," says Dad. "In fact you haven't got any dollars at all."

What he says is true. "All right," I say. "If I prove that there is such a thing as a UFD you have to pay me a thousand dollars. If I can't prove it I will do the washing-up on my own every night for three years."

Dad thinks about this for a while, then he grins and holds out his hand. "Okay," he says, "if you prove there is a UFD you get a thousand dollars. If not—three years of washing-up. You have one week to prove it." He thinks that I am going to back down and say that I didn't see the flying dog. But he is wrong.

I shake his hand slowly. I am not feeling too good though. If there is one thing I hate it is the washing-up. I am sure that no more flying

dogs are going to appear. I do not have the foggiest where the other one came from. Probably Mars or Venus. I wonder if there is a spaceship somewhere looking for it—like in *E.T.*

3

"Come on," says Dad. "Let's go down and get some ice cream for everyone. We only have an hour left before the milk bar closes."

We walk out the drive to Dad's precious new car. It is a Holden Camira. A red one with a big dent in the boot. Dad rubs his hand over the dent and looks unhappy. The dent happened a week earlier and it was not Dad's fault. The boom gates at the railway crossing dropped down in front of the car. Real quick. Dad slammed his foot on the brakes and—kerpow— a yellow Ford ran into the back of our new Camira.

"Ruddy gates," says Dad. He is still rubbing his hand over the dent like it is a personal wound. "Someone ought to report them to the railways. Those gates go up and down like lightning. Don't give you a chance to stop."

Dad is especially sore because there were no witnesses to the accident. No one saw it. If Dad had a witness he might be able to make the owner of the yellow Ford pay up. Now he has to fork out for the repair bill himself.

We drive down toward the milk bar. As we get to the railway crossing I see that there is no sign of any trains. I also see that Mrs. Jensen is about to cross the line with her bull terrier. This bull terrier is the worst dog in the world.

She has it on a long lead. This is good. It means that the vicious animal cannot bite anyone as they walk by.

Mrs. Jensen's bull terrier is called Ripper. This is a good name for the rotten thing. Once it ripped a big hole in my pants. It has also been known to rip holes in people's legs.

Ripper snarls and snaps and tries to get off the lead as Mrs. Jensen walks along.

We are driving behind a big truck. The truckie is looking at Mrs. Jensen's dog Ripper. He is probably glad to be nice and safe inside his cabin. Suddenly the boom gates fall down in front of the truck. The truckie hits the brakes fast. Dad doesn't hit the brakes at all. Our Camira crashes into the back of the truck with a terrible grinding noise.

Dad groans and hangs his head down on the steering wheel. "Not again," he says. "Not twice in the same month." He looks around and then suddenly thinks of something. "Quick," he yells. "Don't let Mrs Jensen go. She is our witness. She saw the whole thing. Run over and get her."

The truckie is getting out. He is a big tough guy.

"Get Mrs. Jensen," yells Dad. "Don't let her go."

I take a couple of steps forward. Ripper is

snarling and snapping. He recognizes my leg. He wants to take another bite.

"The dog," I say to Dad feebly. "The dog will bite my leg."

Dad is looking at the truckie. He really is a big guy.

"Don't argue," says Dad out of the corner of his mouth so that the truckie won't hear. "Get Mrs. Jensen."

I walk over to Mrs. Jensen and her savage dog. "Dad would like to talk to you," I say. "But please don't bring your dog."

Mrs. Jensen is not too sure about this. She does not like me very much. In the end she slips the dog's lead over the end of one of the boom gates so that it cannot get my leg.

A train goes through the crossing and disappears along the track.

The boom gates fly up.

Ripper goes up with the boom gate. It flicks him and his lead high into the sky. Up over the trees and past the kitchen window of our house. His legs are moving like he is swimming in the air. He is yapping as he goes.

4

On the way home Dad is in a grumpy mood. He has one dent in the back of the car and another one in the front.

I am grinning my head off. I wonder how I will spend the thousand dollars.

P.S. Ripper lands in our neighbor's swimming pool. He is last seen heading for Darwin as fast as he can go.

Acknowledgments

For permission to reproduce copyright material acknowledgments and thanks are due to the following:

Tony Bradman: Reed Consumer Books for "Dirty Dilly" from *Dilly the Dinosaur*, Mandarin. Copyright © Tony Bradman 1986. Mark Cohen: Penguin Books Ltd. for "The Case of the Smell" from *The Puffin Book of Fabulous Fables* by Mark Cohen, Viking Kestrel. Copyright © Mark Cohen 1989. Helen Cresswell: Random House U.K. Ltd. for "Posy Bates—Inventor" from *Meet Posy Bates* by Helen Cresswell, The Bodley Head 1990. Copyright © Helen Cresswell 1990. Andrew Davies: Lemon Unna & Durbridge for "Doctor Boox and the Sore Giraffe" from *The Fantastic Feats of Doctor Boox* by Andrew Davies, William Collins Sons & Co. Ltd. 1972. Copyright © Andrew Davies 1972. Anne Fine: Scholastic Children's Books for "Crummy Mummy" from *Crummy Mummy and Me* by Anne Fine, André Deutsch Children's Books, an imprint of Scholastic Publications Ltd. Copyright © Anne Fine 1988. Paul Jennings: Penguin Books Australia Ltd. for "UFD" from *Uncanny! Even More Surprising Stories* by Paul Jennings, Penguin Books Australia Ltd. 1988. Copyright © Paul Jennings 1988. Margaret Joy: Faber & Faber Ltd. for "Miss Mee in a Muddle" from *Allotment Lane School Again* by Margaret Joy, Faber & Faber Ltd. 1985. Copyright © Margaret Joy 1985. Sheila Lavelle: Penguin Books Ltd. for "Harry's Aunt" by Sheila Lavelle, Hamish Hamilton. Copyright © Sheila Lavelle 1985. Margaret Mahy: J. M. Dent & Sons Ltd. for "The Librarian and the Robbers" from *The Great Piratical Rumbustification* by Margaret Mahy, J. M. Dent & Sons Ltd. 1978. Copyright © Margaret Mahy 1978. Jan Mark: Penguin Books Ltd. for "William's Version" from *Nothing to Be Afraid Of* by Jan Mark, Kestrel Books. Copyright © Jan Mark 1980. Andrew Matthews: Peters Fraser & Dunlop Group Ltd. for "Anancy and Tiger" by Andrew Matthews; copyright © Andrew Matthews 1995 and Reed Consumer Books Ltd for "And a Partridge in a Pear Tree" from *S. Claus—The Truth* by Andrew Matthews, Mandarin. Copyright © Andrew Matthews 1989. Bel Mooney: David Higham Associates Ltd. for "But You Promised You Wouldn't Tell" from *But You Promised* by Bel Mooney, Methuen 1990. Copyright © Bel Mooney 1990. Robert Newton Peck: Alfred A. Knopf Inc. for "Apples and Mrs. Stetson" from *Soup* by Robert Newton Peck. Copyright © Robert Newton Peck 1974. Michael Rosen: Walker Books Ltd. for "The Night Thing" from *The Horribles* by Michael Rosen, Walker Books Ltd. 1988. Copyright © Michael Rosen 1988. Irwin Shapiro: Simon & Schuster Inc. for "Strong But Quirky" from *Yankee Thunder* by Irwin Shapiro; copyright © Irwin Shapiro.